THE VAMPIRE KINGPIN

THE VAMPIRE SYNDICATE

REBECCA RIVARD

WILD HEARTS PRESS

1

SPIDER

I followed Velma, my best friend and lieutenant, into an abandoned subway tunnel. We were deep in the Underworld beneath Manhattan, the air heavy with the scent of damp earth and decay. Water trickled down the grimy tile walls, and mold bloomed in reckless patterns on the crumbling concrete.

Velma halted, her shiny black braid stilling along with her. "He's here," she said out of the corner of her mouth. Then, louder: "Grimclaw."

The vampire in question—a sallow creature in a mint-green leisure suit—twitched at the name. Hands buried in pockets, he was trying hard to appear chill, but the stiffness in his shoulders betrayed him. He turned, too fast, eyes sharp despite the washed-out skin.

I jammed a kerosene torch beneath a rusted steel rail and stood back. As my lieutenant, Velma took point on enforcement.

Her hands settled on the long silver daggers strapped over her short red skirt. "We're here for the cash," she told Grimclaw.

He didn't even look at her, his gaze locking onto me instead. Wrong move. Ignoring Velma was the fastest way to get blood on your boots.

"Sorry, bro." He lifted his hands in mock surrender. "I'm tapped out. Next month, you'll get double. That's a promise."

Velma bristled. "That's not acceptable," and the word *acceptable* landed like a blade.

Grimclaw scowled at her from beneath a nest of dark hair. "You can't get blood from a stone."

She snorted, giving a pointed glance to his crotch. "But you're not a stone, are you? You're much...softer."

I chuckled.

Grimclaw's jaw dropped. "Bitch." He puffed up his chest, fangs pricking out between his pale red lips. "Who d'you think you are?"

My chest rumbled in warning. Even in the Underworld, we vampires had a pecking order, and I was the kingpin, the apex predator in this realm of misfits and outlaws, with Velma my beta. This wannabe alpha of a measly crew needed to remember that.

Grimclaw's throat worked. "Sorry, bro. But—"

"I'm not your 'bro,'" I snapped.

"Of course, my lord. I didn't mean anyth—"

Velma yanked her daggers free, the silver a lethal glint in the flickering shadows. "You live down here, you pay Spider tribute. Otherwise, leave. See how long you last."

Grimclaw's gaze darted around the tunnel like a trapped rodent. He knew damn well that anywhere else, his lair would be fighting tooth and nail to survive. I might be a cold-blooded bastard, but I kept my corner of New York peaceful.

He licked his lips. "I don't have the money, but I can get it. I just need a little time. Please, my lord."

"That's what you said last week."

"I know, but—"

I cut him off with a slash of my hand. "Stake him," I told Velma.

"What?" Grimclaw's eyes bugged. Apparently, he'd thought he could keep jerking me around forever. "The hell you—" He dropped into a crouch and whipped out a switchblade.

Velma swatted it out of his hand, and it flew into the gloom, leaving Grimclaw open-mouthed. Even for a vampire, she was fast.

A subtle shift in the air behind us made me spin around. Two members of Grimclaw's lair were creeping along the subway track, blades out.

I let my eyes flash with the blue of my vampire. "Try it," I told them, "and you'll meet the Dark Goddess along with your alpha."

They halted mid-step, throats working.

"Drop. The. Weapons." I threw all my dominance behind the command.

The blades clattered to the ground. "Sorry, Grim," the vampire on the right muttered, hands raised in surrender. "I ain't messin' with Spider. Might as well off my own self and be done with it."

Grimclaw's response was garbled. I turned back to see Velma had pinned him to the wall. She drew back her free arm, dagger poised to strike.

His gaze pleaded with me. "Have a heart, man," he wheezed. "I can pay you, I swear."

"With what?" I returned. "You're tapped out, remember?"

"Not...money. I have something...better. Can we...talk in private?" He was turning purple now, but he managed to cut his eyes at Velma and his men.

"No."

"Please. Trust me. You want...this."

I studied him. The dark gods knew, I was sick of Grimclaw's games, but his lair served a purpose, keeping a far-off section of the Underworld tunnels clear of other supernaturals.

"Let him go," I said.

Velma shook her head but obeyed.

"My lieutenant stays," I told Grimclaw. I didn't trust him not to have more people hidden in the shadows.

He slumped against the tiled wall, sucking in air, but managed a nod.

"Back the fuck off." I jabbed a finger at his men. "But stay where I can see you. You got phones?"

When they nodded, I said, "I want the flashlights on. Shine them on your faces so I know you haven't gone into the shadows."

"Yes, my lord." They withdrew twenty-five yards or so and turned on their flashlights, sending a fat gray rat scurrying deeper into the darkness.

I crossed my arms over my chest. "Start talking," I told Grimclaw. "And make it good, because I've already wasted too much time on your shit."

"It's good." A nervous twitch of his lips. "*She's* good. You're gonna be very...satisfied. I seen you looking at her."

Could he mean—?

My slow-beating heart gave a hard thump. Because this sorry excuse for an alpha did have something I wanted. Very much.

Or make that *someone*.

"Go on," I prompted.

2

LARK

ONE WEEK LATER

I skidded to a stop, the stolen dagger a cold weight against my inner thigh.

At nine P.M., the Village Halloween Parade was just hitting its stride. The streets were packed with dancing, singing Jack Skellingtons, Maleficents, Beetlejuices and other monsters, not all of them human.

Halloween in New York is off the hinge.

But then, so was my cousin Grimclaw's latest scheme. Off the hinge, as in: irrational, demented, no-way-we'd-get-away-with-it.

The real question was, why had I gone along with it?

You didn't have a choice, Lark.

Grimclaw had made it clear that if I didn't steal the dagger, I could find another lair. And who would take in Grimclaw's cousin/stepsister? They'd think I was spying for him. The man wasn't exactly popular in the Underworld.

Dodging a sweaty human in a werewolf pelt, I threaded my way through the crowd until I reached Sixth Avenue.

Steam rose from a subway grate, adding to the Halloween-y vibe. A New Orleans jazz band high-stepped their way past, a gargantuan witch operated by four puppeteers in slo-mo pursuit.

I chanced a look behind me. No sign of Spider, but the skin between my shoulder blades crawled. He was out there somewhere.

He'd *seen* me running away from his lair.

On the other hand, he hadn't seen me with his dagger. That had been safely stowed in a special pocket tied to my inner thigh. Maybe he'd think I hadn't gotten anything and let me go?

Nah. This was *Spider*.

I hadn't just broken into his lair, I'd been in his freaking bedroom. He couldn't let me get away with that.

I swallowed, still tasting the chocolate caramels I'd shoved into my mouth before heading into his bedroom. Big mistake. The time I'd taken to poke around in his lair's pantry had cost me precious seconds, but I hadn't been able to resist dipping into that turquoise MariBelle's box. Living with Grimclaw, I was so cash-poor I rarely had the means to treat myself to really good...anything, really.

And those chocolates had been really, really good.

Twisty the Clown sidled up to me. "Well, hello, Wednesday."

He dropped an arm around my shoulders and toasted me with a can of vodka soda. I stiffened, itching to carve a new smile into his face with my blade. But Twisty was camouflage.

"Hey," I replied in my best deadpan Wednesday Addams.

My costume—black dress with a white collar, hair parted in the middle and braided into two long pigtails—had been chosen to blend in. I'd even powdered my face white to dampen my telltale glow.

Unfortunately, there weren't that many Wednesdays running around, especially bleeding ones. The gash Spider's little trap had left in my palm still hadn't closed—silver wounds take time to heal.

I'd been rinsing my hand in his bathroom sink when I'd heard him outside his lair, talking to a guard. I'd grabbed a handful of tissues, pressed them to my bleeding palm, and faded into the shadows.

I'd escaped, but the shadow world drains you dry, and I'd lingered too long. When I'd dropped back into the physical world, my hand was still bleeding, and trust me, you didn't want to be leaving the scent of blood with a vampire tracking you.

And this wasn't any vampire—this was Spider, New York's Underworld kingpin. The guy was stupid powerful. Even out West, we'd heard of him. I'd wager my (pathetically small) stash of precious stones that he could track me even in a throng like this.

Damn Grimclaw, anyway. Spider wasn't supposed to be anywhere near his lair. Grim had sworn, hand to his black, shriveled heart, that Spider would be out tonight, with only minimal security on duty.

"It's Halloween," Grim had reminded me. "Everyone will be out hunting."

I ground my back teeth. *Thank you very much, Grim.*

It wasn't the first time my cousin had promised something he couldn't deliver. I was the ass for believing him. But in my defense, it *was* Hallow's Eve. We're all—vampires and dhampirs —out roaming on the wildest night of the year. Humans are amped up on adrenaline and alcohol; they practically offer themselves to you on a platter.

Getting into Spider's lair had been easy. I'd only had to evade two booby traps. Then I'd waited in the shadows until one of the men guarding the door had entered the lair and slipped through the door after him. Inside, the lair had been nearly empty.

Piece of cake, right?

But as I opened the wall safe in Spider's bedroom, I'd tripped a third trap, a silver razor that nearly sliced my hand in two. Now I was battling silver poisoning on top of the aftereffects of too much time in the shadows. Both were messing with my ability to heal my palm.

"Great parade, huh?" Twisty yelled in my ear.

I moved a shoulder. "It's…adequate."

"Adequate?" He laughed. "Good one, Wednesday."

My nape tingled, raising hairs all over my body. Spider was near. I *felt* it.

"Later, Clown Boy." Shaking off his arm, I darted under the barricades, ignoring the shout of an irate cop, and shot across Sixth Avenue ahead of a group of glowing skeletons. I ducked under another barricade and pushed my way into the crowd on the far side of the street.

The humans muttered and shot me irritated looks. "Rude," said a woman under her breath.

I flashed my fangs at her. She blinked, then eyed me, interested now. Too bad I didn't have time to play.

Where was Spider?

Scanning the area for a tall, brown-skinned man in a gold-and-brown paisley shirt, I eased backward through the mass of people. Hoping against hope I'd lost him.

The gash on my palm had finally healed over. I balled up the bloody tissues and shoved them into a trash can, hoping to throw him off the scent.

Gradually, the crowd thinned. I sidled up next to a cross-dressing Morticia in towering heels. Maybe Spider would think we were a duo.

Morticia dipped their chin to me, unsmiling. "Daughter."

"Mother," I replied with an equally straight face, pretending interest in the parade at the other end of the block.

A float rolled past, its DJ hyping up the crowd, the heavy

beat of techno bouncing off the brownstones. Footsteps sounded to our left. I chanced a look around Morticia's flowing black dress and caught a glimpse of gold stretched across broad shoulders. He was looking the other way, his brown skin glowing faintly in the darkness like it was moon-touched. A vampire's tell. One that, as a dhampir, I shared.

Hell.

Heart hammering, I attempted to melt into the shadows, even though I was running on fumes. After a few shaky seconds teetering between the physical and twilight worlds, I gave up and ducked into an alley, hugging the wall until I reached a beat-up dumpster. It reeked like something had died in there, but the stench would cover my scent.

Darting around the dumpster, I pressed my back to the gritty brick wall on the other side, taking shallow breaths through my mouth. I palmed my switchblade, wincing as the handle brushed my wound, and wedged myself into the corner made by the dumpster and the wall.

The footsteps halted.

I stilled and held my breath.

The air stirred. Icy prickles skittered up my spine.

The dumpster lid creaked. Spider—because it had to be him—had climbed on top of it. My head jerked up. A man's shadow loomed on the bricks above me.

I bolted for the alley's end.

I didn't make it three steps before he crashed onto my back, taking me to the pavement. The impact drove the air from my body. For a moment, I couldn't breathe. Couldn't move.

Strong thighs straddled my hips. I bucked wildly, trying to throw him off.

Cold silver touched my throat. "You know what I do to thieves?" he said against my ear.

I froze. "I—I—" I dragged in some much-needed oxygen

and wriggled my hips, using the distraction to shove the switchblade back into my pocket.

His blade held steady against my skin, the silver burning like a bee sting. "Talk. Where's my dagger?"

I rested my cheek against the asphalt and rasped, "Don't know."

"Like Hades you don't." He screwed the point deeper, making me suck in a pained breath. "Lie to me again and I'll cut your goddamn tongue out."

I gulped. Jesus, the man was cold. I'd been right to stay out of his way.

He lifted the blade from my neck. "Let's try that again. Where's my dagger?"

"I'm telling you, you've got the wrong person."

Technically, it wasn't a lie. I hadn't said *what* I was the wrong person for.

A harsh sound low in his throat was my only warning before the alley spun around me and I was flat on my back. Spider shoved a blade into a leather holster and straddled my chest. His hands landed on my shoulders, pushing me into the pavement.

He examined me from beneath long, thick lashes. "Where is it?"

I licked my lips, excruciatingly aware of both his knife against my inner thigh and the switchblade concealed in the pocket of the pleated skirt bunched up around my hips.

His gaze went to my mouth, and my mind just...blanked. I'd never seen Spider up close before.

All vampires are gorgeous with an innate magnetism that can scramble your brains. But I was a dhampir, dammit, with some of that beauty and magnetism myself. I should've been immune.

Spoiler alert: I wasn't.

In my defense, the dude was *hot*, with this whole alpha-vampire, I'll-give-you-the-best-fuck-of-your-life thing going on. Liquid brown eyes, shoulder-length hair styled in long twists, a dark scruff covering his chiseled jawline.

But it was more than that. Tall and broad-shouldered, he oozed charisma like a rockstar on stage, commanding attention like it was his right.

He even smelled good. Coconut oil, and something rich and very male. I drew a breath, pulling his scent into my lungs, and his gaze dropped to my flared nostrils.

His sculpted lips tugged up like he was fighting not to laugh.

My cheeks heated. I was *amusing* him.

Working my hands between us, I shoved at his rock-hard abs. "Get off me!"

His eyes tracked from my flushed cheeks to my throat and back to my face again. "Say please."

Something tightened in my core. The way he'd said that...

I was instantly wet. Clearly, it had been too long since I'd had sex.

"What?" I repeated in a too-husky voice.

"You heard me. Beg me, and maybe I'll get off you."

I met his eyes. "Fuck. You."

His face hardened, and he leaned closer, his ropes of hair falling forward to brush my neck and face. The diamond studs in his earlobes glittered like stars against his moon-touched skin.

"D'you know who I am?"

"Um, yeah."

"Then if I were you, I'd start begging."

Alright, now he was pissing me off. Plus, he'd underestimated me because he'd left my hands free. I brought them back to my sides, casually resting my right hand on my rucked-up skirt.

"Make me," I told him, soft and seductive.

His pupils darkened. "Make you?"

Huh. This was almost too easy.

"Mm-hm." I slipped a hand into the pocket and closed my fingers around my switchblade.

His eyes narrowed. "What're you up to?"

"Me?" I released the catch and pulled it out of my pocket, slashing at his face.

His hand shot out, cobra-fast, and plucked the knife from my fingers. He tossed it to the asphalt and slammed back onto me, locking his arm over my throat like an iron bar. "That was a mistake, Lark Nightstar."

When I stiffened at my full name—which no one in the Underworld knew except Grimclaw—a feral smile curved his lips. "Yeah, I know who you are. You think you can live down here for six months without me knowing anything about you? And since you wanna play games, I'm Spider. The man who owns you now."

3

SPIDER

Lark's eyes widened. She pushed at the arm I had clamped over her throat. "Owns me?"

I eased up on the pressure, and she gulped in a breath. "For the next month," I confirmed in a stony voice.

The deal with Grimclaw had been for three nights, but that was before Lark had stolen my favorite dagger, the one forged for me personally. When I'd chased her down, I'd still planned to use her, then send her back to her cousin...minus a finger.

Yeah, she was fetish-sexy in the short black dress and Mary Janes, her shiny dark hair in braids framing a fairy-like face and long-lidded, witchy green eyes. It would be a crying shame to mar that beauty. But nobody stole from me and got away with it.

Then she tried to carve a piece out of me, and damn if everything masculine in me didn't sit up and take notice.

Sexy *and* spunky? Sign me up.

"For a month?" A mixture of shock and defiance battled on her face. "You must be joking."

"No joke." I sat up, still straddling her, and retrieved her switchblade. When it was safely in my back pocket, I fingered

13

her oversized white collar. I recognized her costume now, but the buttoned-up dress and short skirt had a naughty schoolgirl feel that had my dick hard as baseball bat. "I don't joke about things like this. And I could use a new thrall."

Actually, I hadn't kept a thrall in years. But for Lark, I'd make an exception.

Her pointed chin raised a notch. "I'm nobody's thrall. I know my rights—you need my consent."

I eyed her. Was she really that naïve? But no, her tense shoulders told me this was a last-ditch effort to save herself.

"You must be confusing me with a syndicate primus. Down here, I'm the law. If I say you're my thrall, then you are."

The vampire syndicates had inked treaties with the humans to keep the peace and secure a steady supply of thralls for the blood and sex we all crave. The syndicates were big enough and visible enough that they'd had no choice but to negotiate with the humans.

The Underworld, however, was a whole different beast. The vampires down here were outcasts who didn't fit into the syndicates' strict pecking order.

Lark's thick black lashes fluttered. For the first time, I saw fear, quickly concealed.

"But I'm not a human," she said, like that made a difference.

"I know." I brushed bits of gravel from her cheek. "You're a dhampir, and you steal for your cousin Grimclaw. And I can drink from you same as a human thrall."

Actually, a dhampir's blood was superior, the magic in their veins making it more potent. I leaned closer. "And I can fuck you," I added, slowly and deliberately, "same as a human thrall. You stole from me, woman. Now you have to accept the consequences."

"But I don't—I'm *not* a thrall."

"So I'll be your first." I ran my finger down a shiny braid.

"I'll take good care of you. You won't have to risk your life like you do working for your cousin."

Who obviously hadn't informed her of the deal he'd made with me. The man was even more of an SOB than I'd realized.

"But what I do for Grim is my choice," she said. "Maybe I'd rather risk my life than be your *toy*."

She lobbed that last word at me like it would bother me. Instead, it made my dick twitch. Lark as my toy? The word tugged at something primal in me, the part that liked the idea of owning her.

"You should've thought of that before you broke into my lair and helped yourself to my favorite dagger. Now your ass is mine."

She looked a little sick. "I'll give it back then, and we'll call it even. Alright?"

I gave her braid a hard tug. "No."

"Then I'll steal for you, okay? There must be something you want, and I can get just about anything if you give me time." When I shook my head, she said, "Please. I mean it. I'm good. I was trained by the best there is."

"Trained by who?"

A flare of pain crossed her face. "You wouldn't know their names. They were that good."

I frowned down at her, wondering if she meant her parents. When she'd first joined Grimclaw's lair, we'd run a quick check on her, enough to know she'd been raised out West, a part of the syndicate world without ever joining one in particular. Her parents had disappeared six months ago, right before she'd showed up in New York. However, once I'd determined Lark Nightstar was harmless, I'd had Velma stop looking. Down here, we were all hiding something. As long as Lark wasn't a danger to me, I didn't care what the fuck she'd done.

That explained why she was with Grimclaw, though. She

must've had nowhere else to go. And yeah, it bothered me some to realize how alone she was, how desperate.

But I hadn't gotten where I was by being a nice guy.

"I don't need you to steal for me. I have a half-dozen lairs paying tribute." Not to mention my business investments. "So, no. I'll take you."

"But—" She squirmed on the asphalt, reminding me we were still on the hard ground.

I almost apologized for keeping her there so long. My mama, the gods bless her soul, would be rolling in her grave. I muttered a curse and rose to my feet, holding out my hand to Lark.

She ignored it to get up on her own, her right hand held to her side.

I glimpsed the red gash bisecting her palm and grabbed her wrist. "Lemme see that."

"It's okay." She curled her fingers in. "The bleeding stopped."

"I still want to see it." I turned her hand over, examining the palm.

She was right, the wound had closed, but I could tell it had gone deep. I scowled. She shouldn't be risking her life and freedom like this. If she were mine for real, I'd tie her to my bed for a week for a stunt like that.

And that cousin of hers who'd sent her to steal from me? He deserved to be staked.

I released her wrist. "You cleaned it?" The faster you washed out the silver, the less entered your bloodstream.

A nod. "That's what slowed me down. You would've never caught me otherwise."

"Good." I backed her to the wall and slapped a hand against the bricks beside her head. "But just so we're clear, I would've caught you. There's nowhere in this city you can hide from me."

"Whatever." She slumped against the bricks, her face weary

beneath the pale makeup. The silver poisoning must be hitting her hard now.

My jaw tightened. Then some Good Samaritan impulse made me press my wrist to her mouth. "Drink, damn you."

Her eyes rounded. Then she took hold of my arm, her fangs sliding out against my skin. She reared back a few inches, then plunged them into my wrist.

An electric current shot straight to my balls. Sex and blood for us is interlinked. Drinking enhances the pleasure of fucking, and vice versa, especially when Lark hummed low in her throat and sucked harder. My heart gave a thump and my already hard dick started pounding with need.

She felt it, too. Her hips rocked forward, brushing my aching flesh, and her salty musk filled my nostrils.

I was a goddamn saint, because I didn't take her against the wall right there. Instead, I gritted my teeth and reminded myself that she needed to heal from not just the wound but the silver poisoning before we did anything further.

Her sucking slowed. Then she lifted her head and retracted her fangs, lapping at my wrist like a kitten to close the tiny holes she'd left in my skin.

"Thank you," she said. Her color was better, her eyes brighter.

I moved a shoulder, uncomfortable with her thanks, even though it was almost unheard of for a vampire with my dominance to let a dhampir—or anyone, for that matter—drink from me.

"Don't be. I need you in good shape."

"Right." The gratitude on her face faded, leaving me with a hollow feeling in my chest.

"Let's get outta here." I stepped back, glancing up and down the alley. When I looked back, I realized she'd edged sideways.

Maybe I shouldn't have fed her until I had her safely back in my lair.

"Don't. Run," I rapped out.

She straightened to her full height, which was still a good eight inches shorter than me. But the woman had tall energy, I'd give her that.

"Why not? What are you gonna do to me?"

I cupped her throat and pressed her up against the bricks. "Anything I want, little thief. And you'll let me, is that clear?"

She swallowed, the muscles of her neck moving beneath my fingers. The heavy beating of her heart sparked an answering rush in my own veins.

Her gaze dropped, unable to hold mine, but she gamely fought on. "Then I might as well run."

I gave her throat a light squeeze. "Try it."

But I couldn't help admiring her spunkiness. I couldn't think of another dhampir except for the three Kral brothers—and they were high-ranking dominants—who wouldn't have caved in by now.

"Look," I said, stroking my thumb over the soft skin beneath her jaw. "Maybe we can work something out."

"Like what?" she asked warily.

"How about you return that dagger you stole along with an extra ten grand for inconveniencing me, and we'll call it even?"

I was pretty sure she didn't have that kind of cash—as far as I could tell, Grimclaw kept her like some kind of fucking Cinderella, paying her only a minimal wage—but at least she couldn't accuse me of not giving her a chance.

And yeah, I was being a prick, but if she were anyone else, she'd already be in her final grave.

"Ten grand?" Lark's jaw dropped. "Are you fucking kidding me?"

"So you don't have it?"

"Of course not." Her chest heaved. "I don't even have a thousand. Grimclaw takes everything I—" She bit her lip and shook her head.

"So he was the one who put you up to stealing my dagger?"

She briefly closed her eyes. "Yeah."

I grunted. Grimclaw must've realized Lark would never agree to be my thrall in return for his debt, so he'd come up with this steal-from-Spider scheme instead, knowing I'd catch her.

Too bad for Lark, but that didn't mean I was letting her walk. Like I'd said, I hadn't gotten where I was by playing nice.

I traced my fingers up her narrow ribcage, drawing a circle around her nipples with the pads of my thumbs. She dragged in a breath. Her hands came to my chest, her blunt-cut nails digging into my pecs. Her lids drifted down, and beneath the dress's big white collar, the honeyed skin of her throat rippled in a hard swallow.

My mouth watered and my fangs tingled, eager to sink into her pulsing vein, my erection straining painfully against my leather jeans. The blood craving rose in me, fighting to be let loose, to plunge both my fangs and my dick into her.

"Lark," I rasped.

"Mm?" she asked dreamily.

"Look at me."

Her lids lifted, but slowly, as if they were weighted. She blinked at me, then recoiled and knocked my hands from her tits. "Get off me."

With a growl, I grabbed her wrists, twisting her arms behind her back. "Let's get one thing straight. You're not the one in charge here, understand?"

Her witchy eyes flashed, gold and brown lights sparking like fireworks in the green. "So what about working things out? Or was that just a lie?"

"You said you don't have that kinda cash."

"I don't. But I can get it for you. I just need time."

"You sound like your cousin now."

She rolled her lips in. "Please, Spider."

I tilted my head, considering her. She'd stolen from me. As far as I was concerned, I owned her sexy little cat-burglar body now. She was lucky she was still breathing.

But my mind couldn't help flashing to Amina, who'd also pulled a switchblade on a bigger, more powerful vampire, a man who'd wanted revenge on me. He'd snatched her and abused her for three long nights while I tore Manhattan apart looking for her. Then he'd driven a silver stake through her heart. I'd arrived in time to see her body crumbling to ashes. I'd gone berserk, staking him and every last member of his lair, but nothing could bring Amina back.

"Spider?" Lark's questioning tones pulled me back to the present.

I inhaled and focused on her again.

I liked Lark's pluck. She was a...challenge. For the first time in a long time, I felt a spark of excitement for a woman.

Why not negotiate with her? It would be a shame to crush her spirit.

I still intended to take my month, but why not pay her, like I would've any other thrall? When the month was finished, at least I'd have the satisfaction of knowing she'd have enough cash to tell Grimclaw to fuck off.

"I don't need your money," I said, releasing her. "But I'm open to negotiations. Why don't you start by returning my dagger?"

"Sure," she said with a shrug. "Like I said, it wasn't my idea to steal it in the first place."

"How'd you know where to find it, anyway?"

"Grim told me."

"How the fuck did he know?"

"Don't know. But he said it'd be in the wall safe of your bedroom."

I frowned. Had someone in my lair passed the intel to Grimclaw? But who? And why? On the other hand, the existence of my safe wasn't a state secret. It was possible he'd heard about it and guessed that's where the dagger would be.

Then Lark's fingers went to the hem of her dress and I forgot everything but her, my mouth literally watering as she drew the skirt up, high enough that I could see she wore sheer black thigh-highs. I swallowed a groan.

She untied a slim bag attached to her inner thigh and held it out to me. "Here."

I stood, unmoving, watching as her skirt fell back to cover her long, strong thighs. Her gaze lifted to my face, and she stilled at what she saw there.

I took the bag, undoing the strings and drawing out my dagger. As my fingers closed around the familiar, carved ebony handle, a wave of relief swept over me. The dagger wasn't just my favorite weapon, it was my lucky charm.

In the three decades since Amina had given it to me, things had turned around. Lose it, and a superstitious part of me feared I'd lose everything else, too. I only took it out of my safe for special occasions. Otherwise, I kept it locked up.

I slid the dagger into a thigh holster and took Lark's face in my hands. Her heart rate kicked up. I drank in its uncertain, aroused beat.

"Open your mouth," I murmured.

Her throat worked. "Why?"

"Because." I nipped her plump lower lip. "Before we discuss terms, you have to prove you're worth whatever I decide to pay."

At her outraged gasp, I fought back a smile. I tipped her head back with my thumbs, licking the seam of her lips, but her mouth remained firmly closed.

I caressed the underside of her jaw. "Open for me," I told her sternly.

She shook her head, but her hands came to my chest, stroking me like she couldn't help herself.

"That's it," I encouraged. "Touch me like I'm going to touch you."

I moved my mouth to the shell of her ear, tracing it with my tongue. She shivered, and I moved on to her ear lobe, sucking and nibbling. She made a small, sexy sound and gripped the back of my head, pulling me closer.

I brought my lips back to hers, nibbling at her lips. They parted, and I murmured, "Good girl. Open for me."

Her chest shuddered, and with a moan, she sucked my tongue into her mouth.

The dark, primal thing in me reared its head. I deepened the kiss, eating at her hungrily, pulling her higher so she had to come onto her toes. Lark melted into me, one hand around my nape, the other under my shirt, her nails digging into my back, feeding the primal thing with her eager compliance.

I slid a hand between her legs, rumbling in approval when I found all she wore was a silky thong. She widened her thighs, and I pushed my fingers beneath the waistband, roughly caressing her. She whimpered and moved against me.

I backed off, stroking her slow and easy, bringing her to the brink. Then I grabbed her thong to rip it off her. She was so wet I'd slide in easily. I could already feel her closing around my dick, hot and tight...

A burst of laughter jolted me back to our surroundings. On the street, a group of teenaged humans trotted past. I'd actually forgotten we were aboveground, a dangerous lapse with so many supernaturals prowling the Village.

"Spider?" Lark's eyelids lifted.

"Not here," I muttered and reluctantly withdrew my hand from between her thighs.

The dark thing snarled in displeasure, but if I let it out to play, Lark would be up against the brick wall with me buried balls deep inside her—and this wasn't my territory. Yeah, I had an unofficial alliance with the Kral primus based on my friendship with his son Zaq, but I was damned if I'd get caught by a Kral soldier with my pants around my ankles.

Lark dropped back to her heels and stared up at me, her lips reddened, her pupils blown so wide the green was only a thin ring around a bottomless black. She seemed as stunned as I was at what we'd unleashed.

"Let's go." I put a hand on her lower back.

She grabbed my arm. "If I agree, you have to promise me something."

"What?"

"That you'll let me go after a month—that you won't just...keep me."

I took her by the chin. "Now you're pissing me off. Insult me like that again and I'll spank your ass red."

She dropped her eyes. "I'm sorry. I didn't mean to insult you, but...please?"

She'd lost some of her spunk. This meant something to her. She was truly afraid.

"Fine," I heard myself saying. "When the month's up, I promise you'll be free to go. You have my word on it."

She gave me a searching look, then nodded. "Okay."

"But until then," I added, releasing her chin, "I'll take you anytime and anywhere I want."

Her head snapped up. "I haven't said I'll be your thrall."

"Yet," I shot back.

Because we'd already started negotiations, and we both knew it.

4

———————

LARK

Spider hurried me out of the alley and through the West Village. Halloween reigned everywhere. Purple and orange lights adorned the windows, witches flew their brooms in tiny yards and pumpkins glowed on stoops. A human in a devil costume strutted past with a tiny dog sporting matching horns and a cape.

We were five blocks from the parade before I snapped out of my Spider-induced daze.

What was wrong with me?

The man informed me that he owned me and instead of freezing him out, I let him kiss me—and not just a peck on the lips. No, I'd been completely into it. One touch and my stupid body had lit up like one of those strings of Halloween lights. My thong was so wet it rubbed against my clit with every step.

We crossed Fourteenth Street into Chelsea. Spider pulled me into another alley and held out his hand. "Your phone."

"Don't have it," I returned smugly. I'd stowed it in a tunnel between his lair and Grimclaw's in case I got caught.

"Think I'll check anyway. Arms out, legs spread."

"Whatever you say, my *lord*." I flung my arms wide. "But if you wanna feel me up, why don't you just ask nicely?"

Amusement softened his hard mouth. Squatting down, he skimmed his fingers up my thighs inside my dress, lingering on the band of my thigh-highs before moving to my butt, left bare by my thong. His big, warm hands closed on my naked cheeks.

He gave a hum of appreciation. "You do have a sweet ass, Lark Nightstar."

My throat worked. This time I made myself stay still. But my pussy clenched, completely on board with whatever he had in mind, the scent of my arousal drenching the air.

He picked up on it, of course. A vampire's senses are ten times as keen as a human's. He went motionless. Then he lifted his head, his dark gaze burning into mine from where he crouched at my feet.

Electricity arced between us. The back of his fingers brushed the crotch of my thong, sending a shock of pleasure radiating up my spine. He found my clit and rotated a knuckle over it.

"Very sweet," he added in a husky murmur.

I briefly closed my eyes. Then I fisted my hands and deliberately looked past him. "Are you finished?"

"Yeah." He stood back up, a small, we-both-know-you-liked-it smile playing on his lips.

I waited for him to call me on it, but he just said, "C'mere," and before I knew what was happening, his long fingers were wrapped around my head, holding my face to his broad chest.

"What now?" I grumbled, voice muffled, and tried not to breathe. This time, I was *not* going to notice how good he smelled.

"Hush."

I couldn't see what he was doing with his other hand, but a few seconds later, a door creaked open behind me. Interesting. An entrance to the Underworld I didn't know about.

"You first." He indicated the opening with his chin.

I obeyed, accepting that for now, I was his prisoner. At least he wasn't Jared Darkman.

Spider sent a last look up and down the alley, then followed me onto the flimsy metal landing. Darkness enveloped us.

He glided past me. "You can see?"

"Yeah," I said, my eyes adjusting to the low lighting.

"Stick close. The rats know not to mess with me." He started down a flight of sketchy-looking stairs.

I jogged after him. "I'm not afraid of rats."

I'd even made friends with a couple of them—the only friends I'd made in Grim's lair. At least the rats I could trust.

We descended two flights. At the bottom, the murkiness swallowed us whole—too thick even for our night-adapted eyes to penetrate. Spider flicked on a tiny flashlight, revealing an ancient subway tunnel that looked like it predated New York City itself—cracked white tiles, dank pools of water. We continued, picking our way over the rotted wooden ties beneath our feet.

A flash of movement made me look down—directly into a pair of beady red eyes. I automatically reached for the handful of dried corn I usually kept in my jeans, but since I was wearing a dress, I came up empty-handed. Unfortunately, this skinny, beady-eyed dude didn't seem to have heard about the rats I'd befriended outside my cousin's lair.

"Good boy," I said weakly.

Spider threw a look over his shoulder. "Don't worry, he won't bother you."

"How d'you know? That guy looks hungry."

"Probably 'cause he is."

"Not helping," I muttered, and I could've sworn he stifled a laugh.

Then, to my relief, he bared his fangs and hissed at the rats.

The darkness exploded with a half-dozen rodents emitting furious squeaks and scattering.

I may have let loose with a girly squeak myself. "Jesus, I hate how they travel in herds."

"Herds?" He made a choking sound.

He was definitely trying not to laugh.

"Glad I'm amusing you," I said dryly. But this time it didn't bother me—in fact, for some damn reason, I was proud of myself.

"It's called a mischief." Spider started walking again, me sticking to him like Velcro.

"A what?"

"A mischief of rats."

"No kidding? Fits."

"Anyway, chill. A light will go on right about—" A kerosene torch flared to life, scorching my eyeballs, and another half-dozen rats darted off. "Now," he finished, turning off the flash-light and tucking it into a pocket.

With the rats gone, I couldn't help appreciating the view prowling down the track ahead of me. His leather jeans and silk shirt molded to his sinewy frame like they'd been sewn on him. The man had the perfect ass for leather—firm, hard-muscled.

Maybe being his thrall wouldn't be so bad...

I wrenched my gaze from his ass, irritated at myself.

He stopped and took my hand, his fingers warm and firm. "Bend your knees."

I complied, crouching and walking sideways like him until he released my hand and straightened up.

He slanted me a look. "You'll have to tell me how you got around our traps."

"Sure." I smirked. "But it'll cost you. Ten thousand oughtta do it."

He snorted.

A second kerosene torch flared on, making me blink against the brightness.

Spider indicated a wooden tie. "This one you have to jump," he said, springing a good yard above the track to clear it.

I rolled my eyes. "Like I can jump that high," I said—and executed an aerial somersault instead, landing on the tie next to his.

His thick dark brows climbed. "Starting to understand how you evaded our traps."

I grinned up at him, and his rich brown eyes crinkled in return. Suddenly, he seemed like a different man. Someone I could...like.

My heart thumped. I dragged my gaze away.

Put the brakes on, Lark. The man literally threatened to cut out your tongue for lying to him.

He tucked a stray hair behind my ear. "You're not what I expected."

"Yeah?" I lifted a brow. "I'm better? Smarter? Freakin' fabulous, in fact?"

His low chuckle sent an answering vibration through my lower belly. His mouth opened, and I stilled, convinced he was going to say something crucial.

But he didn't. Instead, he closed his mouth and continued down the tunnel, once again the stern Underworld kingpin.

And no, that wasn't disappointment I felt.

The entrance to Spider's lair was a giant iron door crisscrossed with silver straps to repel vampires. Spider greeted the guards in an undertone. They eyed me suspiciously while he spun a trio of cogs set into the iron in a quick pattern, his hands moving too fast for me to catch the sequence. The door swung open to reveal a large, communal space that was a blend of modern tech and fantastical steampunk-y elements like iron pendants with Edison bulbs that cast a warm glow.

I'd been here earlier, of course, but at that point I'd been focused on the job. Now I took in the comfy leather couches, the pool table, the wide screen TV and the thick rugs covering the slate floors. Curtains in warm oranges and reds softened the stone and concrete walls, and a couple of antique trunks serving as coffee tables were piled with magazines and books. At the opposite end of the room was a kitchen with a long wooden table for the dhampirs and humans in the lair.

Envy chewed at my insides. This lair was a home, something I'd never really known. Even when my parents were still alive, we were always moving, always scheming, seeking the next big score.

And Grimclaw's lair had *never* felt like home. It had just been where I laid my head.

Spider glanced at me, and I had a feeling he could read some of what I was feeling on my face.

I pulled back my shoulders. "Nice crib."

"Thanks. We call it the Cavern."

"Not the Web?"

"Too obvious," he said, and even though he didn't smile, I could've sworn I felt his mood lighten a little. "You know where my bedroom is," he added with a nod at the door beyond the kitchen.

"That's where we're negotiating?"

"It's private," he said, even though the Cavern was completely empty.

When I hesitated, he put a firm hand on the small of my back, steering me through the room and past the kitchen.

His bedroom was a lush retreat done up in velvet and silk. He closed the door and went to his wall safe, which in my hurry, I'd left cracked open, and returned his dagger to its inlaid wood box. He put the box back in the safe along with my switchblade and spun the combination lock, clearly not worried that I'd already demonstrated I could break into it.

"Sit down." He sprawled on the black velvet armchair next

to the bed, long legs stretched out before him, his twists flowing around his face and shoulders like a coffee-colored lion's mane. "Before we talk terms, let's get a few things straight."

I perched on the edge of his massive bed, hands behind me on the black-and-gold silk comforter, and crossed my ankles all demure-like. I could act like a lady when it suited me. "Like what?"

He traced a hot-eyed gaze over my legs. "First, you're not a guest here. You have the freedom of my bedroom and the Cavern, but go anywhere else and the guards will have orders to toss your ass in a cell."

I dug my fingers into the comforter. "Like fuck, they will. I'll be out of here so fast your head will spin."

His eyes flashed. He came out of the armchair and crossed to me in a single, sinuous movement.

I straightened and put my feet on the floor. But I was damned if I'd let him lock me up. I might as well have stayed in Vegas and let Jared Darkman make me his blood slave.

Spider inserted a knee between my legs, forcing them open so he could step between my thighs. He took me by the shoulders and pulled me up.

"Don't push me," he said, soft and dangerous. "Because I will hunt you down and make you sorry. That's another promise for you."

I swallowed hard. "Grimclaw will—"

"Turn you over to me. Haven't you figured it out yet? That's why he sent you here in the first place. He owes me a month's tribute, but he doesn't have it, so he sent you instead."

"Are you serious? He fucking sold me?"

"Yeah. We made a deal. I get you, and he gets another month protection."

A ringing filled my ears. "He wouldn't—"

"No? Want me to text him for you?"

I stared up at Spider's too-handsome face, wishing I could

accuse him of lying, but it sounded like something Grim would do. I'd tried to make myself valuable to him and his lair, but if it came down to saving his own skin and protecting me, he'd drive a knife into my heart himself.

It still stung. Grim was family. With my parents gone, he was all I had left.

I drew a breath, recalling a snippet of conversation I'd overheard last week between him and his creepy lieutenant, Troll. I caught my name, and "Spider." Then they saw me and clammed up.

When Grim had ordered me to steal the dagger, I'd figured that was what they'd been plotting. But now I realized the whole thing had been a setup, a way to deliver me to Spider. Grim had known I'd never agree to be traded for the money he owed Spider. I'd made it crystal clear that I'd never let him pimp me out. So instead, the SOB had sent me into Spider's lair, knowing I'd get caught.

And I'd walked right into the trap like a trusting, overconfident rabbit.

"Well?" asked Spider.

I shook my head. "Don't text him," I said around the lump obstructing my throat.

It's okay. You don't need that asshole. You don't need anyone.

Spider swore under his breath. He released my arms to cup my cheeks.

"That fool doesn't know what a gift you are. If you were mine, I'd never risk you by sending you up against someone like me."

My mouth twisted. Somehow, Spider's sympathy made me feel worse. Maybe because it drove home how completely alone I was.

"What are these terms of yours?" I asked gruffly.

He released my face and undid the first three buttons of my

dress. Opening the collar, he stroked a finger down the hollow of my throat.

My pulse hammered, and his focus went to it.

"You'll belong to me. No other men. I'm the only one who drinks from you. The only one who fucks you."

I tried not to squirm, but it was the way he said it—dark-edged, low and commanding. I was still upset, but maybe becoming Spider's thrall would have...benefits.

He skimmed a finger beneath my bra, teasing my nipple. "I'll treat you good, I promise."

He tweaked my nipple, and a buzzing filled my brain.

I knew I should be negotiating, but my palms raised of their own accord. I ran them up the rounded muscles of his shoulders, learning his feel. Lower down, I pressed against his erection, blindly seeking relief from the aching need.

With a muttered curse, he dragged up my skirt. A big hand clamped on my bare ass, holding me in place so he could grind himself against my mound, the only thing between us his leather jeans and my flimsy thong.

A twist of his hips, and sparks went off all over my body. I swallowed a groan and twined a leg around his upper leg, trying to get even closer.

"Fuck." Sharp teeth closed on my earlobe. "You want this, dammit. Just say yes and I'll bend you over that armchair right now."

A wicked heat shot straight to my sex. My breasts felt full... achy. I squeezed my thighs together, picturing him bending me over...taking control of me.

"You'll belong to me. No other men. I'm the only one who drinks from you. The only one who fucks you."

I screwed my eyes shut, lightheaded with lust.

Yes. Sweet Luna, yes...

I opened my mouth to agree—anything if he'd take the ache away.

Until it hit me that he was manipulating me, using my body to get me to agree before we set terms.

The man was clever—everyone said so. Maybe this was his way of getting around making an agreement with me.

A wave of fury made me hiss. I pushed on his shoulders, arching away from him. So. Damn. Angry.

At myself, for being so weak.

At Grimclaw and Spider for bartering me like I was a package, not a person.

I was even angry at my parents for taking too many damn risks until they got caught and left me alone in the world.

"But I don't want it."

He growled and slapped my ass. "That's a lie."

"If you say so, my *lord*."

A sharp-toothed smile. "Is that supposed to piss me off? Because I like it when you call me 'my lord.' I also answer to 'master' or 'sir.'"

I turned my head so I wouldn't have to see his hard, beautiful face. "In your dreams."

His head lowered, his teeth scraping over my neck, a tiny punishment that made me shiver—and hate myself for it.

He licked the small abrasion. "So mouthy. But I can feel your heat even through my jeans. And we both know you're wet for me..."

He rocked his engorged dick against my mound, slow and easy. I bit back a whimper as he hit a perfect, sensitive spot.

He chuckled darkly. "Yeah, you really hate this, don't you?" He ground himself against my swollen flesh, pulling a desperate cry from me.

That. Right there.

"Say it. Say you want it."

"Yes," I whispered, unable to help myself. Gods, I was spineless where he was concerned.

"Louder," he said, his expression implacable. "So we both know you mean it. Say that you want me to fuck you."

I shook my head.

"Then we'll stop." He put me a little away from him, forcing me to unwind my leg from around his and release my grip on his neck.

I squeezed my thighs together, so aroused I was trembling, and balled my hands into fists. "You're a dick, you know that?"

"Yeah—so? Now tell me you want me to fuck you."

"Fine! I want you to fuck me."

Triumph flashed across his face. He reached for me, but I held up a hand, backing up. Luna knew I wanted him. I *needed* to feel him moving inside me.

However, I was my parents' daughter, too.

"But not," I added in as firm a voice as I could manage, "until we agree to terms."

"You wanna know what I'll give you?" Somehow, he was right in front of me again. He ran his hands up my arms. "Pleasure," he husked, low and suggestive. "A safe place to stay. A comfortable bed."

Longing surged within me.

It was like Spider knew I hadn't felt safe since my parents got themselves staked six months ago, caught trying to con Jared Darkman, the son of the Vegas primus. I escaped and found my way to Grimclaw, who'd never joined a syndicate. He'd taken me in, but it was a devil's bargain. Yeah, he'd given me sanctuary—not that Grim knew I was on the run—but he'd exploited my debt to him, even going so far as to command me to steal Spider's dagger.

Moreover, I was constantly on the lookout for his lieutenant, Troll. A hulking figure from Jersey who made Tony Soprano look like a choirboy, Troll had tried to coerce me into his bed. He'd only backed off because of my cousin. But in the past couple of months, he'd renewed his attempts to catch me alone, until I'd moved out of the main lair. Now I slept in a four-by-ten-foot cubbyhole with a switchblade under my pillow, and made sure I was up and gone before Troll woke from his day sleep.

"Lark?" Spider's brows drew together. "Where'd you go?"

Panic clawed at my lungs. I pushed his chest. "I can't think. Let me go. *Please*," I added belatedly.

He immediately released me. Giving me space, but I saw the hunger sharpening his face.

I braced for a fight. "I need...time. I have to think. Or are you going to force yourself on me?"

"Force you?" His mouth tightened.

I stepped back, wrapping my arms around myself. At my closed posture, he squeezed his nape.

"Fine," he bit out. "You can have a night to think it over."

I relaxed a little. "Thank you."

"Oh, you *will* pay me. Nobody steals from me, little thief. Now, how about a blood-wine?" He moved to a beautiful ebony wet bar at the other side of the room. "You're still too pale."

I rubbed my upper arms. "I spent too much time in the shadows."

"Huh. That's how you got in the door?"

I dipped my chin.

He frowned. "The guards should've been more careful."

"The door was only open for a few seconds—not sure what they could've done." I brought my arms back to my sides. "And...I'd rather have a blood-whiskey. If you have it, that is."

His gaze snagged mine, probably seeing it as the small surrender it was. Then he nodded and pulled out a bottle of thousand-dollar blood-whiskey and two old-school whiskey glasses—rugged and no frills, with a thick base.

He poured a generous amount of whiskey into both glasses and passed one to me. "Cheers."

"Cheers." I raised my glass to him. The liquid shimmered darkly under the dim light.

Spider clinked his against mine, and we sipped at the same time. I felt him looking at me, but I avoided his eyes.

The whiskey slid down my throat like liquid fire before mellowing into a much-needed magical heat that spread throughout my body. It was almost as good as Spider's blood.

"You like?" Spider asked.

"Oh, yeah."

I took another sip. A droplet of whiskey remained on my lips and I flicked my tongue out, drawing it in.

When I glanced at him, a muscle in his cheek was working. "One night," he growled. "That's it."

He waited for my nod, then said, "I have to run. Here's something to wear." He tossed me a T-shirt. "Help yourself to something to eat, or another whiskey. Whatever's gonna bring some color back to your face. And Lark?" His face hardened. "Steal from me again and the deal's off. I'll chop off your goddamned hand and send you back to your cousin."

I lifted my chin, the T-shirt clutched to my chest. "I won't, as long as you're straight with me."

"Then we won't have a problem. Now, be good."

And he was gone.

I stared at the closed door. Then I finished my drink and took up his invitation to find something to eat. The Cavern was still empty so I fried up a couple of burgers, downing them between gulps of another blood-whiskey. In the walk-in pantry, I helped myself to two more chocolates. Might as well eat my fill of MariBelle's while I could.

My mind flashed to my cousin's lair where food was something you had to scrounge up for yourself, and I felt another pinch of envy. By then, most of the silver had worked its way out of my system, and between that and a full belly, I could barely keep my eyes open.

I wasn't sure where I was supposed to bed down, but Spider had ordered me not to leave the area, so I made my way back to his room, where I took a quick shower in his beautiful, blue-and-green tiled walk-in shower, putting my hair up and letting the hot shower pound my sore muscles from five different directions.

Before leaving the bathroom, I rinsed out my thong and thigh-highs and draped them over a towel bar, claiming territory in my own small way. Back in his bedroom, I pulled on his T-shirt and crawled into his king-size bed along with a paperback mystery I found on his dresser. The bedding smelled like him.

I snuggled deeper and sighed at how comfortable I felt. How safe.

Troll couldn't sneak up on me here; I could allow myself to relax.

I cracked open the book—and promptly nodded off, stirring only when Spider returned and took the open book off my chest. He killed the light and climbed into bed, slinging a heavy arm over my waist.

I roused enough to mumble, "Didn't know where to sleep."

"Right here, little thief." He nipped my nape. "You're exactly where I want you."

When I opened my eyes again, it was late afternoon and my nose was pressed to Spider's neck, my arm and thigh thrown over his naked body like I was trying to burrow into him. I remained there for a long minute, absorbing that *you're-safe* vibe into my bones.

Don't get used to it. People like you don't stay in one place—and men like him aren't safe.

I slid out from under the covers.

First things first. I retrieved my blade from his wall safe, telling myself I was only taking back what was mine to begin with.

I glanced at the blade, then at Spider. The comforter had slipped down, baring his neck and one powerful shoulder. Even in sleep, he looked dangerous, a lion at rest.

But he was a lion with an Achille's heel, because I could stake him and slip out of the Cavern in the shadows.

My gaze flicked to my palm. The gash was barely visible, and I felt better than I should've after a silver cut that deep. I licked my lips, recalling Spider's rich, masculine taste, his power obvious in how rapidly his blood had healed me.

He'd done that for me when he didn't have to. He could've let me suffer—I'd deserved it for breaking into his lair in the first place. But instead, he—an alpha vampire—had allowed a low-in-the-hierarchy dhampir to drink from him.

Confusion balled in my stomach. What was the dude's game?

I didn't understand him, and that bothered me.

Whatever happened, I was done with my cousin. I was *never* going back. I was sick of being jerked around and treated like a servant, not a full-fledged member of his lair.

I'd known for a while that I had to get out, but Grim had kept me on a tight financial leash, taking whatever I stole as payment. Room and board, he called it, even though I brought in thousands each month.

When I'd balked, he'd let Troll search me. The prick had put his beefy hands all over me until I'd been forced to cut him. He would've beat me if Grim hadn't intervened out of some belated cousinly feeling. After that, I handed the jewels over without argument. I couldn't afford to get kicked out of Grim's lair. The only safe place for me was the Underworld.

My parents had had money, but I didn't dare try to access it. Jared Darkman would be watching their accounts. My only assets were a pair of ruby earrings and a matching necklace—all I'd had with me when I'd left Vegas.

So why not agree to be Spider's thrall? It's not like sex with him would be a hardship.

I wouldn't do it for free, of course. The man had money. He could pay me.

And then I'd be out of here.

A tendril of uneasiness slithered up my spine.

It might not be that easy.

I shrugged the uneasy feeling off and headed into Spider's bathroom for another shower. This time I washed my hair, shaved my legs with his razor, and helped myself to another shirt—an expensive silk button-up. I rolled on the thigh-highs and stepped into my low black boots. The blade went into a sheath on the inside of my left boot.

Only then did I venture into the large cavern to scare up something to eat. A couple of women and a man were seated at the kitchen table, eating bacon and eggs. They stilled mid-bite and turned in unison to stare at me.

I froze, recognizing the guards I'd sneaked past—the man, a loose-limbed, curly-haired, golden-skinned dude, and the shorter woman, a lean redhead with a pixie cut and freckles. Like me, they were dhampirs, but the other woman was human. The emotions leaking from her—dislike and suspicion—gave her away.

"Hey." I pulled up an easy, I'm-harmless smile. "I'm Lark."

"We know," the dude replied, his sharp brown eyes sweeping over me in a quick, assessing look.

"Right." Of course, Spider would've told them about me.

He indicated the platter in front of him. "You hungry?"

I forced my tense shoulders to ease. Stay smooth, my dad would've said. Never show the cracks.

"Starving," I admitted with a self-deprecating grin.

The redhead pointed a thumb at her chest. "I'm Zayne.

That's Jacko." She tipped her head at the curly-haired dude. "Plates are in the cabinet by the coffee pot."

"Thanks." I got out a plate and silverware, helped myself to a mug of coffee and sat at the table, leaving a seat between me and the other, taller woman.

She eyed me from beneath a straight black fringe. "I'm DeeDee."

"Nice to meet you." I dug into my food. "This is good," I said around a mouthful of buttery scrambled eggs.

Jacko preened. "Thanks."

"So, Velma says you're Spider's new thrall," said Zayne.

I took a gulp of coffee. "Velma?"

"Spider's lieutenant," Zayne replied.

"Oh. Well, I guess you could say so." I suspected they knew I was actually his prisoner, but maybe they didn't want DeeDee to know.

"Are you or aren't you?" asked DeeDee.

I moved a shoulder because it wasn't any of her fucking business.

She didn't take the hint. "If you're not his thrall, then what were you doing in his bedroom?" she demanded.

I met her eyes. "Because he wanted me there."

DeeDee's dark brows came together in a perturbed V. "He doesn't sleep with thralls. Says he doesn't trust them. We usually don't even keep them."

I couldn't decide if she was jealous or merely protective. "Well, he slept with me."

"Let it go," Zayne told her. "She wouldn't have been in there if Spider wasn't okay with it."

DeeDee frowned at me but subsided.

I continued eating. Zayne tried to draw me out, so I gave her enough to get her off my back, saying I'd grown up out West but had joined Grimclaw's lair in April.

"Grimclaw?" Jacko asked, exchanging a look with Zayne.

"It's temporary," I muttered, embarrassed to admit I was part of the shakiest lair in the Underworld. "As soon as I can, I'm out of here."

They nodded and, to my relief, let it go.

Brunch over, I offered to clean up the kitchen. DeeDee left for a job on the surface—she was a bartender, apparently—and Zayne and Jacko had guard duty. They helped me carry the dirty dishes to the tub-sized, stainless-steel sink, then leaned in from either side of me.

A sharp point touched my spine. I stopped in the act of reaching for the bottle of dish soap. "Something wrong?"

"Spider wants you to stay put," Zayne said. "We have to patrol the tunnels, but we'll be checking in on you."

"You leave," Jacko added, "and we'll know it. Just in case you have any ideas about escaping."

"Got it." I calmly drizzled soap over the plates and turned on the water to fill the sink.

The pressure on my spine disappeared, and Zayne squeezed my shoulder. "I think I'm gonna like you. Tell you what—I'll dig up some clothes for you. We're around the same size."

"Yeah? That'd be lit."

"No problem," she said, and Jacko chimed in, "Later," and they strolled out of the Cavern.

Blowing out a breath, I finished the dishes, then flipped through a couple of magazines before returning to Spider's bedroom. I sank into the armchair and waited for him to wake up.

5

SPIDER

I came out of my day sleep to the *snick-snick* of a switchblade. I tensed, preparing to launch myself out of the bed, until Lark's scent hit me, a blend of my shampoo and her own unique essence.

I turned my head. My soon-to-be thrall slouched on the chair next to my bed, her legs draped over one of the velvet-covered arms, playing with the blade I'd taken from her. Behind her, my weapons cabinet was open. She'd also gotten into my closet because she wore my favorite purple silk shirt over the thigh-highs from last night.

The *snick-snick* ceased. "You're awake."

"Mm-hm," I said without taking my gaze from where the thigh-highs disappeared beneath the tails of my shirt. Was she wearing the thong under that?

She got up, smooth as a cat. "I'll stick around," she informed me, "but on my terms."

Now we were getting somewhere. I leaned back against the headboard, fingers laced behind my neck. "Spill."

The sheet bunched at my waist, leaving me bare from the waist up. From the way she moistened her lips, she liked what she saw. The feeling was mutual. I'd come awake with morning wood but at her obvious interest, my dick tried to drill through the damn sheet.

She took that in, then moved her gaze up...slowly. Taking in my chest. My biceps. And finally, my face.

"One month," she told me. "At the end of that time, my debt is paid—and I want an extra fifty grand on top of that."

I lifted a brow, enjoying myself more than I would've expected. "Now why would I agree to that?"

She strolled the few feet to the bed and leaned over. The purple shirt gaped open, giving me an eyeful of small, perfect tits. Her shiny black hair spilled forward to brush my chest.

Behind my head, my fingers clenched, itching to gather that silky mass and guide her soft mouth down to my cock.

"Because." She traced the point of her blade down my sternum and past my navel. Her *silver* blade, which meant it left a trail of fire. "I'll be the best fuck you ever had."

The pain only made me want to force her down on the bed and teach her manners. Just picturing it made me harden even more.

She used the point to flick the sheet draping my dick, threatening me in a way that I shouldn't have allowed. But I let her get away with it. The woman had cast a fucking spell on me. I was this close to saying to Hades with negotiations and just giving her whatever she wanted if she'd come back to bed.

I didn't even think she was exaggerating. I suspected she *would* be the best I'd ever had.

But it went against the grain to allow her to get the upper hand, and I was pretty sure she'd lose all respect for me if I gave in so easily.

"No to the fifty grand." I nudged the blade away by its steel, nonpoisonous-to-vampires handle. "You owe me those thirty nights. You broke into my lair and stole from me. Anyone else would be in their final grave."

"You have your damn dagger back." Closing the switch-blade, she slid it into her boot and crawled on top of me, her long hair tickling my chest and abs. "And we both know you can spare the Benjamins."

With a feline look at me from beneath her lashes, she licked her way from my belly to my chest in the opposite direction she'd drawn her blade.

"You're going the wrong way." I reached between our bodies to shove the covers away. My dick sprang free, brushing her stomach.

Her warm fingers closed on me. I had to grit my teeth to keep from groaning aloud.

"Forty thousand," she said.

"Ten," I managed to say, my gaze on her strong, elegant fingers.

She gave me a slow stroke up and down. "Twenty-five."

I gathered Lark's silky locks in my fist and pulled her head back. "Done."

Her beautiful eyes narrowed. "Thirty nights, and you'll pay me twenty-five thousand dollars?"

"Yes."

"Swear it."

My hand tightened in her hair. "That's the second time you doubted my word. You'll get your twenty-five, damn you. Now show me how good you can be."

Her witchy eyes lowered. "Yes, my lord."

Oh, the woman was going to slay me. Probably literally.

But what a way to go.

"*Now*," I told her.

She tightened her fingers around my root but took her time lowering her head, drawing out the anticipation, teasing me with small licks and nips until I growled, "Take me inside your mouth."

Pursing her lips, she blew warm air on my engorged head.

And then finally, mercifully, her lips covered the cap, teasing the slit with her tongue, licking the pre-cum weeping from me.

"Like this?" she asked around me before sucking me deep inside.

Every muscle in my body locked. "Fuck, yeah. Just like that."

She hummed in pleasure. An answering vibration tightened my groin.

Without pausing in her rhythm, she straddled my left thigh. Her wet sex brushed over my bare skin, answering the question of whether she was wearing a thong.

She wasn't.

Her free hand slipped lower, caressing my stones. Both my hands were in her hair now, guiding her up and down.

She started moaning and riding my leg, grinding her dripping pussy against my thigh, letting me know how much she liked me controlling her...ordering her around.

"That's it," I told her. "Get yourself ready for me. Touch yourself."

Releasing me, she slid her hand between her spread legs. I silently damned myself for not having her remove the shirt first, because the fabric blocked my view of her tits.

I cupped her head and thrust inside her mouth. The base of my spine clenched, my balls drawn up with the need to explode.

"You gonna swallow, pretty thief?"

She hummed an assent, the vibration sending a wave of pleasure crashing over me. I gave several hard thrusts, then abruptly changed my mind.

This first time, I wanted to be inside her, taking her hard while I drank from her vein, my mouth filled with the flavor of Lark. I owned her now, and I wanted her to feel it.

I tugged her hair. "Stop."

She murmured questioningly against my skin. When she

raised her head, her green-and-gold irises were outlined in neon blue, her vampire-half staring up at me.

"Too much?" She smiled, a seductive, I'm-a-predator stretch of her lips—and let her fangs slide out, toying a sharp tip with her tongue, testing to see what I'd allow.

I smiled back, and extended my fangs as well. Unlike Lark, I intended to use them—on her.

Our gazes snagged. I let my own eyes spark blue, a wordless warning that if she pushed me too far, there would be consequences.

Still toying with the tip of her fang, she tipped her head to one side like a sexy, black-haired kitten. Then her fangs slid back into her gums.

I released her hair. "Take off the shirt."

She came up on her knees, drawing the shirt over her head and tossing it on the chair, leaving her dressed in nothing but the boots and thigh-highs. Her hair fell in a midnight waterfall around her shoulders.

My lungs stopped up.

In my three decades as a vampire, I'd seen some fine-ass women. None of them came close to Lark with her creamy olive skin and strong, graceful body, her full lips wet from sucking me, her tits round and topped with dark-rose nipples.

She started to crawl off me, but I grabbed her by the hips, stopping her so I could give each of those pretty nipples a hard suck.

Her head fell back in pleasure. She wrapped a hand around my nape. "Do it again—harder."

"Please," I prompted against her breasts.

She growled under her breath, but obeyed. "*Please.*"

When I complied, her free hand moved down her stomach toward her pussy.

"No touching." I gripped her wrist, halting her.

Her lush mouth formed a pout. "Why not?"

"Because I'm the only one who gets to make you come." I scraped my fangs down her neck.

She inhaled. "That hurts."

"But you like it."

"Yeah," she admitted.

I licked the small scrapes to soothe them. "Good girl."

"Why?"

"For telling me the truth."

"I don't lie," she returned. She waited a beat, then added, "Usually."

Fuck, she was adorable. I grinned against her temple. Still, I couldn't let that "usually" pass.

"Make that never when you're with me," I told her, and lifted her off me, setting her on the mattress.

"I'm not making any promises."

"I can promise I'll spank you if you lie."

"Only if you kiss it better when you're done," she shot back.

"Depends on the lie." Crawling on top of her, I took her mouth with mine, then moved her closer to the bronze headboard. "Grab the rails and don't let go."

"Yes, sir." This time, she wasn't teasing me. Keeping her eyes on me, she reached up, one hand at a time, and wrapped her fingers around two thick rails.

I removed her boots, dropping them on the floor, then pushed her legs apart so her knees were bent up, and made my way down her body. Biting and sucking and licking until I reached her mound. Her tits lifted and fell, her hips moving restlessly on the sheets.

I rubbed my cheek over her wiry dark curls, then buried my face between her thighs. She smelled incredible. Earthy and feminine.

I cupped her ass, giving her rounded cheeks a good squeeze, and licked up her slit, teasing her swollen clit with my tongue and lips.

"*Spider*." My name came out on a rough exhale. "Yes. That..."

I did it again, and she moaned, her fingers opening on the rails.

I scraped my teeth along her inner thigh, warning, "Let go and I'll stop."

"No!"

"Then do as you're told."

A jerky nod. Her hands tightened around the rails so hard her knuckles whitened.

"You know what I'm going to do?" Without waiting for a reply, I brushed my thumb back and forth over her clit. "I'm gonna drink from you. I'm hungry." And I craved her taste like a junkie needs their next fix.

She tensed beneath me. "I never..."

"That's what I thought." The primal part of me loved that in this one thing, she was still a virgin. "But you'll let me, won't you?"

I slid a finger into her pussy. The muscles contracted.

She hissed, her hips jerking. "Oh, gods..."

I sucked her clit, pumping my finger and out. "I've got you, baby. But tell me I can drink. Tell me you want it. I promise I'll make it good."

I nibbled her clit, and she nearly levitated off the mattress. Then, chest working, she nodded her head.

"Out loud," I prompted. "I need your words."

"I want it, okay?" Her teeth sank into her plump lower lip. "I want to feel your teeth. I want...everything."

My belly tightened. I couldn't remember the last time I was this eager to fuck a woman. I was literally humping the bed.

I licked her thigh, drawing in her delicious, fuckable scent. I had two fingers in her now. She was clenched tight around me.

"More?" I pumped my digits in and out.

"Yes, please." She turned it into a chant. "Please, please,

please..."

I extended my fangs and plunged them into her thigh. Her flavor exploded into my mouth.

The aphrodisiac from my saliva entered her bloodstream at the same time and she wailed, high and unintelligible. Her cunt clamped around me, over and over, as she came on my fingers.

My mind blurred with a dark pleasure. But I didn't drink— not yet. This time was about her. I'd promised it would be good, and like I'd told her, I kept my promises.

I licked the tiny wounds, sealing them, and as she went limp with the aftermath, I crawled on top of her. "Turn over."

She drew in a jagged breath, then came onto her hands and knees looking like something out of a dirty movie, all smooth curves and sheer black stockings.

My hand landed hard on her bottom. "That's for stealing from me."

"I'm sorry," she gasped out.

"Too bad." I spanked her again. "You're still in trouble."

She pushed her ass up to me, wordlessly asking for more. "I'm sorry," she mumbled, dropping her head so her forehead was on the sheet. "I won't do it again."

"Let's make sure." I gave her several more slaps while she squirmed on the mattress, babbling an apology. When her behind was nice and warm, I slid my fingers between her legs, rubbing her clit. She was wet from the punishment and her orgasm.

"Now I'm gonna fuck you," I said against her ear. "Keep that ass up for me."

I waited for her nod, then grabbed a condom from the nightstand. As supernaturals we didn't have to worry about STDs, and it was rare to knock up a woman who wasn't your mate. Even so, I was always careful to wrap up.

Returning to the bed, I positioned myself behind Lark. Taking her by the hips, I dropped a kiss between her shoulders, then pressed into her, a slow, sweet glide that made my jaw clench with sheer pleasure.

She squirmed to get even closer to me, and I forgot about being slow, thrusting into her hard. Her hand crept between her legs.

"Dirty girl," I said against her nape. "Touch yourself. Make yourself come for me."

Her soft-skinned ass writhed against my groin. "Harder."

I liked her begging. I slowed my strokes again. "Say please."

When she just shook her head, I bit her shoulder, and she arched her back, a raw cry escaping her lips.

"What do you say?" I prompted.

"Please. *Please.*"

"Please what?"

"Please...fuck me," she said, interspersed with gasps as I pushed forcefully into her. "I like it...hard."

"You got it, baby." I raised up and smacked her ass.

Her breath sobbed out.

I took a fistful of her hair, pulling her head back so her throat was exposed. She tensed, panting. I knew she was nervous but at the same time, her pussy clenched on me.

I stilled, quivering like a damn racehorse, as, very slowly, she angled her neck, giving me better access. Blood hunger darkened my vision at her wordless submission.

I zeroed in on the turn of her shoulder. Her external jugular should be just...about...there. The primal part of me took over, shocking in its intensity. My mouth opened, my fangs fully extended. I reared back, preparing to strike at her neck like a fucking rattlesnake.

She whimpered, the sound penetrating my fevered brain enough to rein me in. I struck, but in slow motion.

She cried out, her back bowing and pressing her ass into my lap. My mouth filled with her rich, salty taste. I swallowed and thrust into her roughly, steeped in her flavor and scent.

She shuddered, her sex clamping around me. She was coming already. I pumped into her, keeping up that rough, hard rhythm until her contractions stilled and her head lolled forward.

My rational part nudged me. Take any more, and I might harm her, especially after that gash she'd gotten on her hand yesterday. I reluctantly withdrew my fangs and licked the small punctures until they closed up, then flipped her onto her back.

I came back between her bent legs and threaded my fingers through hers, pressing her hands on either side of her head and putting my tip at her entrance. She looked up at me, flushed and beautiful, her eyes clouded, her inky hair spread over the sheets.

As I pressed into her, I groaned. "Gods, you feel good."

A smile curled her kiss-swollen lips. "Told you."

And damn if I didn't like that she could still tease me. My usual thralls would've been promising me anything by now, but not Lark. She was both submitting to me and pushing back. Making me so horny I wanted to spank her ass again for being so...perfect.

I wasn't in complete control, and that scared me.

Normally, I could keep going for hours, feeding and fucking. But my body was demanding release. I thrust inside Lark, deep and hard, then stilled. Attempting to regain my self-discipline.

"More." She arched her back, her stiff nipples brushing my chest. "Make me come again."

I curved above her so I could give each of her rosy tits a hard suck. "This time, I'm coming, too."

She gave a throaty moan and reached up to kiss me. "Yes," she said against my lips.

My already frayed control tore with an almost audible rip.

I started pounding into her, riding her so hard, she moved

up the bed, her head coming dangerously close to the metal headboard.

I released her hands. "Grab the rails."

She quickly obeyed, holding herself steady to meet my demanding thrusts, hips lifted and knees wide open to take me.

With each stroke, I rotated my hips so that the base of my dick rubbed her clit. Somewhere far back in my mind, I wondered what in Hades had come over me.

She's just a thrall.

But her pleasure had become as important as my own. I wanted, no *needed*, to give her an earth-shattering climax, to see her eyes go blind with ecstasy.

In the end, it was me who went blind.

She released the rails to dig her nails into my ass. "More," she sobbed out. "Please... *Harder.*"

I willingly gave her what she was begging for. Her inner walls contracted, milking me tightly. I caught a final glimpse of her face, contorted with pleasure/pain, then my vision hazed and all I could do was feel her and smell her.

I snarled and slammed into her again and again until a climax exploded through my system like a heat-seeking missile. Beneath me, Lark cried out—high, sexy sounds that mixed with my own agonized groan.

When I came back to myself, I was hanging over her, my teeth open on her shoulder. Not hurting her or feeding from her.

Just...holding her. Claiming her.

I recoiled, guilt constricting my chest. I'd left tiny red marks on her smooth skin, marking her in a way I hadn't done since Amina.

Quickly, I withdrew from her body and rolled onto my back.

She released a shaky exhale. "Holy shit."

I mentally agreed. That had been intense. So good, it felt like a slap to Amina's memory. My almost-mate. The woman I'd intended to claim before that rat-faced punk had staked her to get back at me.

Velma had said Amina wouldn't want me to feel guilty.

I wasn't so sure. Amina had loved me as hard as I'd loved her. If she'd found me in bed with another woman, she would've carved off my stones with a dull knife.

But Amina had been in her final grave for twenty-one years now. She wouldn't have liked it, but she would've accepted it, just as I would've understood if the situation had been reversed.

Having sex with Lark wasn't the problem here. It wasn't even wrong to enjoy it.

What bothered me was that for the first time in two decades, my brain had been wiped of any thought of Amina, a woman I'd vowed never to forget.

I'd broken that vow because all I'd been able to think of was Lark.

Taking her.

Pleasuring her.

Keeping her.

I turned my head to find Lark looking back at me. Her lips lifted in a soft smile. "Hey."

Something jagged tore into my chest. The guilt ratcheted up, along with a touch of panic. Time to pull back before she got the wrong idea.

This couldn't be anything else. I wasn't keeping Lark, even if I hadn't promised she could leave after the thirty days were up. Nobody could replace Amina. I'd resigned myself to a life without a mate.

"Thanks." I planted a casual kiss on her mouth. "You got skills, woman. That twenty-five is looking like it'll be worth every dime."

"Oh. Right." Her smile faded. She rolled her lips into her mouth. Then she formed them into a lopsided grin. "Guess I should've held out for fifty."

6

LARK

Mortification heated my cheeks. I dropped an arm over my face, praying Spider wouldn't notice.

I'd *begged* him. Allowed him to drink from me. Let him take me anyway and anyhow he wanted—and I'd loved every second of it. I was still humming.

Yeah, I talked a big game, telling him I'd be the best he ever had. But he'd flipped it on me, because he'd turned out to be the best I'd ever had. A fairy tale come to life, except in this version, the villain pleasures the woman until she forgets he's no prince.

Problem was, when it was over, I'd forgotten *why* we were tangled in these sheets. That I was Spider's thrall. That this was a hustle, me grabbing a chance to score some easy cash.

Worse, he'd known that I'd forgotten. That I'd been feeling...feelings. Warm and fuzzy, *I-could-like-you* feelings.

I'd seen his expression. He'd felt sorry for me. Hell, he'd looked guilty.

I cringed inwardly. Talk about an icy slap of reality.

What was wrong with me? Lark Nightstar didn't *do* feelings.

Feelings were messy. They bogged you down, trapping you more effectively than silver chains.

I'd forgotten myself, that's all. It had been a long time, and I'd been horny.

Now, though, I wanted to grab my clothes and get the fuck out of Dodge. But even if Spider would've let me out of our agreement, I needed that money. It represented freedom, a fresh start.

No, I'd stay the whole month, even if it killed me.

"I should've held out for fifty."

At least I'd dredged up a smart-ass comeback, saving myself from complete humiliation. Maybe he'd figure he'd read me wrong.

And yeah, his relief had been obvious. But that was good, right? It meant we were both on the same page.

Spider rose from the bed, disposing of the rubber before padding naked to his weapons cabinet. "You can keep your switchblade," he said as he locked it back up, "but open this cabinet again and I'll stake you myself."

Stake me? Ohh-kay.

"Got it," I said, sitting up.

Message received, loud and clear: *Don't make this something it's not. You're nothing to me.*

I wouldn't make the same mistake again. I'd enjoy the hell out of sex with Spider, then take his cash and book it out of here.

Yeah, it hurt. But bruises healed. The key was to protect yourself and avoid further damage.

And it's not like my heart was bruised. He'd only poked my ego.

I swung my legs to the floor, suddenly desperate to scrub his scent off my skin, and grabbed the purple shirt. "Are we done here? Because I could use a shower."

A hesitation. Then he said, "Sure."

I felt his eyes on me as I sauntered naked to the bathroom. Glancing over my shoulder, I was pleased to see his brow furrowed. What, did he expect me to break down and cry like some human virgin?

I blew him a kiss and closed the door on his confused face.

When I remerged, wearing his shirt and my clean thong, the door to the Cavern was open. Spider had pulled on a pair of boxer briefs and was speaking in an undertone to a tall Amazon of a vampire with a thick black braid and a pair of lethal-looking daggers strapped over her short orange skirt.

"This is Velma," he told me. "My lieutenant. If I'm not around, she's in charge."

"Nice to meet you," I said.

She acknowledged that with a short nod and turned back to Spider. "I'll look into it. For now, I'll be out on patrol."

"I'll catch up to you later," he told her.

As Velma left, Zayne popped into the doorway. "Hey, Spider. I have some things for Lark." She indicated the stack of clothes in her arms.

"Thanks." He glanced from her to me like he was wondering how I'd made a friend so fast. "I'll give them to her."

As he took them, I leaned around him to thank her myself. "You're a sweetheart."

"No problem," she said with a warm smile and left.

Spider shut the door with his foot. When I tried to take the clothes, he held them out of my reach, feeling each piece of clothing—leggings, a couple of T-shirts, an exercise bra and a handful of panties and socks.

It took me a few seconds to realize he was searching for a weapon. I blinked. "You don't trust Zayne?"

"I trust her, alright." He dropped the clothes on the bed. "Just being careful. And if I didn't, I wouldn't tell you."

"Got it." I blanked my expression. "Sorry if I overstepped."

His mouth pressed into a tight line. Then he said, "Get

dressed and help with dinner. You wanna eat around here, you work."

I moved a shoulder. "Fair enough."

He considered me like he couldn't quite figure if I was gaming him.

"I mean it," I said. "I appreciate you feeding me. And I'm no princess—I don't need to be waited on."

He grunted and disappeared into the bathroom. A moment later, I heard the shower go on.

I got dressed in a gray tee and black leggings, then stacked the rest of the clothes in a corner of the bedroom. By the time Spider came into the Cavern, I was in the kitchen slicing tomatoes for Croc, a short, bulked-up human with cropped hair and a wicked scar curving from his left eye to his cheek.

Spider frowned as Croc (short for Crocodile) gave a rusty chuckle at my lame tomato joke. (Why did the tomato cross the road? *To ketchup with the other tomatoes.*)

It was almost like Spider was jealous. His hand went to the handle of the dagger in his holster, and he actually took a step toward us before giving himself a shake. He turned on his heel and strode out of the Cavern.

I frowned after him, then shrugged and went back to my tomatoes.

"These babies are almost done." Croc flipped the burgers he was broiling for the ten or so other humans and dhampirs who'd drifted into the Cavern. "You finished with those tomatoes?" When I nodded, he put me to work washing lettuce and chopping carrots for a salad.

THAT'S how things went for the next few nights. I slept in Spider's bed each day, waking up first and waiting for him. We fucked. That part was incredible—easiest money I'd ever made.

Then I helped cook, and we ate family-style around the long wooden table, humans and dhampirs side by side. In addition to Croc, Zayne, Jacko and DeeDee, I met a couple of other dhampirs—a teenager with bright blue hair and a dark-skinned, silver-haired dude, among others.

No thralls.

When I asked Bliss, the blue-haired kid, about it, she said, "You're the only one. Usually we feed from our humans, or hire someone for the night. We pay them as we go, or barter with them."

"But then why did he—"

"Hire you as a thrall?" she finished. "We're all wondering that."

"I guess he figured he couldn't get you any other way," said Monster, the silver-haired dude.

I swallowed hard. Even before I'd extracted the extra twenty-five grand from Spider, he'd been willing to take me in place of the twenty-five Grim owed him.

Somehow, it hadn't hit me before now that Spider must've wanted me—bad.

And why did that give me that warm, fuzzy feeling again? I quickly smothered it?

Chill, Lark. He wanted in your pants, that's all.

Everyone was listening now. From across the table, DeeDee sneered. "Soon as the month's over, he'll kick you to the curb."

"That's the deal," I agreed with a shrug.

She looked taken aback like she'd expected me to be upset. But then, she didn't know that I'd been the one to insist that my deal with Spider had an end date. She wasn't finished, though.

"After he lost Amina," she informed me, "he swore never to take a mate. Just so you don't get ideas."

"He had a mate?" That good feeling I'd gotten from hearing how much Spider had wanted me popped like a soap bubble. I'd assumed that like me, he'd never mated.

She widened her eyes in a show of innocence. "You didn't know?"

"It wasn't official." Zayne interjected from the head of the table. "He never claimed her. And I think that's enough about Spider," she added with a frown at DeeDee.

The human sent me a sulky look from beneath her black fringe.

"Thanks for the intel," I told her. "But I'm not doing this for free, you know." I took a big bite of my hamburger, another Croc special with onions, mushrooms and melted gorgonzola cheese.

She blinked and Zayne let out a laugh. "That's your answer," she told DeeDee, who pursed her lips.

As for me, I was savoring my hamburger. "Damn, Croc," I said around a juicy mouthful, "this is good. That gorgonzola is genius."

A flush crept up his thick neck. "Thanks."

I chewed slowly, grateful for the human half of me that allowed me to feed on something other than blood, alcohol and chocolate. Yeah, vampires were hella powerful with longer lives than a dhampir, but I preferred having a foot in both worlds.

DeeDee renewed her attack. The woman had a raging hard-on where I was concerned.

"Cut the act, already. We all know you're a plant. Grimclaw's been eyeing this lair for a decade. You'll run back to him and spill all our secrets. Next thing we know, we'll all be dead."

Grim had been eyeing Spider's lair?

But it made sense. My cousin would never have the resources—or the balls—to build something like this.

"DeeDee." Jacko crooked an arm around her neck in a firm hold. "Shut it, okay?"

She stiffened. "Sure, take her side."

"It's cool," I said peaceably. "I get that I might look like a plant. But don't you think Spider's smart enough to figure that out?"

On cue, the man himself appeared in the Cavern doorway, his twists pulled into a casual ponytail, a soft green T-shirt stretched across his broad shoulders. "Smart enough to figure what out?"

DeeDee shot me a nervous glance.

Jacko released her. "Told you to put a lid on it," he muttered.

Much as I would've liked to stick it to DeeDee, I wasn't a snitch, and I didn't know Spider that well. If I told the truth, he might punish her. Hell, Grimclaw would've backhanded us both for bitching.

But I took my time answering. Let the chick sweat.

Spider sauntered across the room. "Lark?" His hands landed on my shoulders. He gave me a warning squeeze. "What's going on here?"

I licked my lips. "I was just telling DeeDee and everyone that I'm only sticking around for a month. After that, I'm outta here. No way I'm going back to Grimclaw's lair. I'm leaving New York."

"And why am I smart enough to figure that out?"

"Because you know I'm not a local—and why would I stay after what Grim pulled?"

Man, I used to be slicker than this. Growing up with a pair of smooth-talking sharks as parents had been a master class in evasion. But somehow I couldn't lie to Spider, not when he'd made it clear that lying to him was a deal-breaker. So, every word was the truth.

"Hm." Above me, I felt Spider studying DeeDee. "Is that right?"

Her mouth puckered like she'd swallowed a lemon. "Yeah."

"I see." His grip on me eased, and I went still, fearing this was the calm before the storm.

But he just told her sternly, "Well, listen up. Lark is here because I want her to be. You respect her, or you'll answer to me."

DeeDee's gaze dropped to the table. "Yes, my lord."

Spider added, "That goes for all of you."

The others nodded or shrugged. I released a breath and fought back a big grin. The last thing I'd expected was that Spider would take my side against anyone in his lair, even a human.

He put a hand on Monster's chair. The dhampir sprang up, asking, "Need a seat?"

"Appreciate it."

Spider sank into the chair and yanked mine close, his muscular thigh touching mine. Velma, who'd watched the whole scene with an unreadable expression, moved to the entrance, turning her back to the room to keep an eye on the tunnel beyond.

DeeDee got up and brought Spider a glass of blood-wine. He accepted it with a smile that said she was forgiven. The group visibly relaxed.

You could tell they were tight, swapping stories and laughing together. Spider toyed with my ponytail while I listened, that envy constricting my chest again.

These people were family, their lair a place where both humans and dhampirs could drop their guards and be themselves. I'd never had that, except with my mom and dad. When you're always on the move, switching up identities because the old ones got too hot, you can't make real friends.

The meal over, other vampires drifted in, dropping onto the couches along with the humans and dhampirs who weren't helping with clean up or on guard duty. Spider pulled me to him for an open-mouth kiss, saying, "I'll be back," before leaving with a couple of the vampires he didn't bother to intro-duce to me.

Feeling out of place and a bit lonely, I grabbed a towel and helped dry the dishes and put them away, even though Croc told me I didn't have to since I'd helped with dinner prep. When the kitchen was clean, I lingered on the edges of the gathering, debating if I should wait in Spider's bedroom like I had the past couple of nights. But that wasn't my style.

So when Zayne, Jacko and Monster gathered around the pool table next to the wet bar, I made my move. "Mind if I join?"

Monster's deep-set brown eyes gleamed in anticipation. "You any good?"

I lifted a shoulder. "I can hold my own."

"It's fifty a game."

I wrinkled my nose. "I don't have any cash."

"No sweat." He handed me a cue stick. "I'll front you a hundred bucks. You and me will play first, then Jacko and Zayne. The winners play for the pot."

7

SPIDER

Grimclaw smirked knowingly. "So how do you 'like' Lark?" He made an obscene gesture, making it clear what he meant by *like*. "Maybe you wanna keep her another three days? 'Cause I'm open to negotiations."

My mouth tightened. When Jacko had reported Grimclaw lurking near the Cavern, I'd gone out to meet him. Time to get a few things straight.

Beside me, Velma shifted her weight and put her hands over her daggers—a not-so-subtle threat. She'd never liked Grimclaw, and with her background, knowing he'd bartered his own cousin to pay his debts made her firmly Team Lark, despite her doubts about my new thrall and her connection to Grimclaw's lair.

Grimclaw's leer faltered at our twin glares, but he kept running his mouth. "She's worth a year of tributes, right? Not that I'd know personally, but that body. And the chick can *move*. I bet she can twist herself into a pretz—"

"Shut it." I got right up in his grill. "Lark's mine now. You don't get to talk about her. I don't want you to even fucking *think* about her. She's dead to you, understand?"

As far as I was concerned, Grimclaw had lost any claim to Lark when he'd bartered her without her agreement.

"That wasn't the deal," he sputtered. "Y-you can't just steal her from me! I'll tell everyone—"

"You'll say nothing." I shook him by the throat. "Because if you do, I'll put it around that you sent her to rob me. I should stake you for that, but I got Lark out of it. She's worth your life —for now—but keep pushing and I'll forget to be nice."

His mouth opened and shut like a fish.

I released his throat. "And you owe me last month's tribute. The deal was off as soon as you went after my dagger."

His eyes flashed blue, and a switchblade jumped into his hand. "You goddamn double-crosser. Fuck your tribute."

I snarled and grabbed his wrist, slamming his forearm down over my thigh. He grunted in pain and dropped the blade.

Before he could recover, I had him up against the moldy concrete wall. "You motherfucker—tell me why I shouldn't end you right here."

His eyes bugged out like a cartoon rabbit. "I—please, my lord. I'm sorry. I—it's just Lark's family."

Like he cared. He wanted the money she brought in.

Velma pressed against my shoulder, her thick black braid falling forward over one breast, and slid a dagger between me and Grimclaw.

She dug the point into his crotch. "Let me cut him."

He gave a girly shriek and tried to cover himself with his hands. I grabbed his wrists and forced his arms open, kicking his legs apart so he was spread-eagled against the wall.

"Spider." His eyes pleaded with me, man to man. "You can't let this bitch cut—"

"She's my *lieutenant*," I interrupted. "Call her a bitch again and I'll let her do anything she fucking pleases to you."

Velma muttered in satisfaction.

"She doesn't like men who sell women," I added. "They trigger her."

Grimclaw licked his lips. "I'm sorry, okay?" This time his pleas were directed at Velma. "I apologize if I insulted you."

"Too late, asshole." She cut a slit in the material next to the placket of his tight pants. "Lark's your cousin, a member of your lair. You're her alpha."

"Not anymore," I broke in.

"You *were* her alpha," Velma corrected herself. "You're supposed to protect her, not barter her like a piece of meat. You deserve to be punished."

Her blade stabbed inside the slit she'd made in Grimclaw's pants. He went rigid, coming up on his toes with an agonized groan.

"No, don't," he said, high and fast. "Please...I'll get you the money. Whatever you say. Just please don't cut me."

I swallowed a grimace. It was instinctive, like Velma had touched that honed blade to my own dick, but I let her do her thing. She might be damaged—she'd been held captive by blood slavers for close to a year before I'd stumbled upon their lair and rescued her—but she had iron-hard control.

"You *will* get Spider his tribute," she informed him. "But this is for Lark."

Her hand jerked. Grimclaw's scream echoed down the tunnel.

Velma and I released him, and he crumpled to the ground, hands over his crotch, the scent of his blood mixing with the dank air.

My lieutenant curled her lip. "You'll be alright. I didn't do anything permanent. But I will fucking neuter you if you ever try and pimp another woman."

Grimclaw flashed her a look of hatred, quickly concealed.

"A week," I told him. "You have one week to make your payment, or you're out of here."

His head snapped up. "You'd kick me outta the Underworld?"

"Fuck, yeah. You're a piss-poor alpha. I can't believe you haven't been staked in your sleep with the shitty conditions you keep your people in."

"Fine. You'll get your damn money."

"My lord," Velma prompted.

His mouth formed a thin line. "My lord," he mumbled.

We'd made an enemy there. I could live with that; the fool wasn't much of an ally anyway, too weak to be a decent alpha. Even if he came up with the money, his lair was going to implode within a year. When they did, they'd turn on each other like a pack of starving dogs.

Lark was lucky to be out of there.

"I'll expect my tribute next Sunday," I informed him. "And again on the first of December."

I strode off, Velma on my heels, leaving Grimclaw whimpering and muttering to himself.

We got back to the Cavern to find Lark bent over the pool table, her dark hair in a high, shiny ponytail, her round butt on display in black leggings. And Jacko and Monster weren't the only dudes eyeing her like they'd enjoy a bite.

The meeting with Grimclaw had left me on edge, ready to fight—or fuck. Her tiny gray tee had ridden up, exposing a strip of smooth skin just above the leggings. My fangs pressed at my gums, my mind flooding with X-rated images of yanking down her leggings and hauling her back on my waiting erection. Laying claim to her in front of all the men eyeing her sexy backside.

She nailed her shot, sinking the eight ball. She rose back up, shooting me a *Damn, I can't believe I made that* smile over her shoulder.

Like she wasn't hustling my lair.

It made me swallow a chuckle even as I ached to take her. And the best part? I could.

I prowled across the lair. She kept her back turned to me, eyes on Monster as he racked the balls for the next game. But I could tell she was clocking me, tracking my every move. She struck a pose, hand on the wall, one hip cocked, like she was daring me to come after her, to demand her attention.

I slid up behind her, hands on her hips, and scraped my teeth down the side of her neck. A little shiver went over her, and beneath the form-fitting tee, her nipples hardened into points. I skated a hand up her abdomen, stopping just short of her breasts, and she stilled, then arched her back so her ass was pressed against my thighs, my dick nestled in the small of her back.

I spread my fingers over her stomach, keeping her up against me. "Lemme guess," I said to Zayne, Jacko and Monster. "She's hustling you all."

Jacko released a crack of laughter. "She's up eight hundred bucks on us."

"What?" Lark leaned sideways so she could see my face and shot me a shameless grin. "I need the cash."

Zayne rolled her eyes. "She played fair. It's not her fault these dudes figured they could beat her just because she has tits."

"Not true!" protested Jacko. "You beat me just last month, and you have tits."

"And I fronted her the cash to get in the game," Monster grumbled.

I dipped my head, closing my teeth over her earlobe. "Say goodnight, Lark. You're done here."

"Yes, sir." She did a little swish-swish of her hips against my thighs. The top of her ass brushed over my erection and I bit back a groan. "Just let me get my money—"

"Here." Monster scooped up the stack of bills and handed it to her.

I released her, watching as she peeled off two fifties for him. "Thanks for staking me."

"Anytime." The usually poker-faced dhampir smiled back. "Where'd you learn to play like that, anyway?"

Lark tucked her winnings into her bra. "I was home-schooled. Had a lot of time."

Which didn't really answer the question. But if there was one rule in the Underworld, it was Don't Ask Too Many Questions. We all had our secrets.

Monster slid the fifties into his billfold. "You'll have to give me a few pointers."

My new thrall quirked a brow. "But then I'd have to kill you."

Monster blinked, then let out a belly laugh that had heads turning all over the Cavern. I was as surprised as everyone else. The silver-haired dhampir rarely even cracked a smile.

Lark grinned. "Just kidding. I can give you pointers."

"Tomorrow," I cut in, snagging Lark around the waist. "Later, y'all."

I made a beeline for my bedroom, but of course, it wasn't that easy. First one person, then another stopped me with questions that just couldn't wait. I concealed my impatience because it was part of being an alpha, but I kept Lark snugged up against me and dealt with their problems in as few words as possible. Finally, we were in my room, the door shut behind us.

I spun Lark so her back was against the thick wood. "You're so bad."

"What?" she asked, all wide-eyed innocence. "You have a problem with me playing pool?"

I rested my forearms on either side of her head, caging her in. "Hustling my crew, you mean?"

She scrunched her nose at me. "You heard Zayne—I played

fair. I can't help it if they're willing to bet against someone they've never seen shoot a ball."

"Then we don't have a problem. They're big boys and girls. They lose money to you, that's their funeral. But if you wanna make friends, you might let them win once in a while."

"I suppose so—and I did promise to give Monster some pointers. But what does it matter? I won't be here long enough to make friends."

Discomfort moved through my chest. I didn't want to think about how limited our time together was. Three days ago, thirty nights had seemed like plenty to get her out of my system, but now I wasn't so sure.

"You could stay," I heard myself say. "After the month is over."

"As your thrall?"

"As a member of my lair."

"Really?" She blinked up at me. "I-I don't know what to say."

I frowned. I'd figured she'd jump at the chance to join my lair. "Say yes. You have skills," I added. "We could use a woman like you."

"Right." Her eyes shuttered. "Look, I really appreciate the offer. I mean, you don't even know me."

That was true, and it wasn't like me to be so impulsive. On the other hand, if I wanted to keep her out of Grimclaw's clutches—and I'd meant every word I'd said to him—why not offer her a place in my lair? And I could certainly use a woman with Lark's skills.

Yeah, right. You want her for her 'skills.'

I could almost hear Amina's dry tones.

The woman who'd been staked when I'd misread a situation, pushed a rival alpha too far.

The woman I'd vowed would always come first.

Up until now, that had been easy. No one else had ever come close.

But I didn't want to think about that now. Not with Lark's small, perfect breasts pressed against my chest, her beautiful face inches from mine. I kissed her to shut us both up, gratified at how her fingers dug into my shirt as she opened her mouth to me.

I deepened the kiss, sliding my tongue over hers, nibbling at her lips.

She twined a leg around my thigh, urging her center against my aching ridge of flesh. I tore my mouth from hers, moving it to just beneath her jaw. I latched onto the tender skin, sucking hard enough to leave a mark.

When I raised my head, I informed her, "I'm gonna bend you over my chair, just like you were over the pool table."

She huffed a laugh. "You liked that, huh?"

"Oh, yeah." I smacked her ass. "You don't wanna know what I was thinking."

"No? Try me." She waggled her dark brows at me.

My mouth twitched up. I couldn't help it. She was a wild card, continually surprising me. When I expected her to back down, she amped things up, making me smile. And fuck me, but I liked it.

"I wanted to bend you over the pool table right in front of everyone. Pull down your pants. Wrap your hair around my fist." Sliding the hair tie from her ponytail, I sank my fingers into her satin locks. "Like this."

Her eyelids drooped. Her lips parted. "I—"

"You wanna know why?" I asked against the side of her neck.

The smooth muscles of her throat moved. "Why?"

"So I can control you as I ride you. So you know exactly who's making you come."

"I'll know," she said with an eager hum that sent an

answering vibration into my chest. She worked her hands beneath my shirt, smoothing them up my rib cage, then scraping her nails down my nipples to my navel in a shock of pleasure/pain. My dick swelled, threatening to bust out of my pants.

"Touch me." I took her hands and brought them to my erection, molding her fingers around my needy flesh.

She took over, stroking and squeezing. "You're so big," she breathed, which made me want to strut like a fucking peacock.

"Because of you." I rubbed myself against her palms. "I've been ready for you since I woke up. And Lark?" I teased her nipples with my thumbs. "It's gonna take me hours with this fuckable little body of yours before I'm satisfied. I hope you're up for that."

She twined her arms around my neck and pressed her body against mine. "Bring. It. On."

Our mouths met, clung, our tongues dancing with each other. When we broke apart, we were both breathing hard.

"Clothes off," I said and stripped her myself, needing to keep my hands on her.

She snatched the cash from her bra before I could touch it, and then glanced at me. "It's yours," I told her.

She jerked her head in acknowledgment and shoved it into the pocket of her leggings while I dragged off my clothes.

I pushed down my comforter. "Sit on the bed."

She perched on the edge of the mattress, hands on either side of her hips, her hair falling over one creamy shoulder. I stepped between her thighs. Her breath caught, the movement lifting her high, pretty tits.

Her eyes lifted to mine. "What about bending me over the armchair?"

So she'd liked that idea. "We'll get to that." I wrapped my fist around my erection. "But first, I'm gonna lick you. Make sure you're ready for my cock. Any objections?"

She gave a quick shake of her head, her gaze on my slowly pumping hand.

I used my free hand to stroke a thumb over her glistening pink center. "You're already wet for me, aren't you? Or are you like this because of those men out there?"

When she didn't answer fast enough for me, I paused, my palm resting on the dark curls of her mound. "Answer me or I'll stop."

Her face jerked up. "No! Yes! I mean—it's you. I'm wet for you."

"Good. Because I'm the only man who gets to fuck you tonight." I gave my dick a few more hard pumps, then released it and, putting a hand on the bed next to her hips, slid two fingers into her.

She fell back onto the bed, braced on her forearms, watching me through lowered lids, her teeth digging into her lower lip. "So good." She swiveled her hips against my fingers, seeking more. "Feels so...damn good."

"Mm." I withdrew my fingers, rubbing the knuckles, slick with her juices, over her clit.

She moaned and my stomach clenched. I loved how quickly I could rev her up.

I slid my fingers back inside her, thrusting them in and out a little roughly. "What did you think about while you were playing pool? Were you sticking that sexy ass out for those other men in the Cavern?"

The idea made the primal thing a little crazy. I didn't want her to want any other men. It was mixed up in her past connection with Grimclaw. That she'd run to a guy like him for help instead of coming to me.

I knew that wasn't reasonable—how could she have known I'd help her?—but that's how I felt.

When she took too long to answer, I bit her hip bone hard

enough to leave a mark. She gasped and clamped down on my fingers.

I pumped them into her again. "Answer the question."

"No. I wasn't. I swear!"

"Then what were you thinking about?" I ghosted my lips over her clitoris.

"Nothing, damn you."

I made a harsh sound low in my throat. "Do I have to stop? Because I think you're lying."

"Fine. I was thinking about you, alright?" Her head tilted back, her ebony hair spilling onto my sheets. "You're stuck in my brain."

That was real. I felt her growing wetter, smelled the spike of arousal my demanding questions created in her. The primal thing quieted.

"Yeah? Think about this, then." I swirled my tongue around her clit. Sucked strongly.

Her hips bucked. "Yes, yes, yes," she said, the words slurred.

A few more licks and sucks and she was writhing beneath me, her thighs shaking.

I backed off. "Say please."

I wanted her begging and incoherent. No, scratch that.

I didn't *want* her begging and incoherent. I *needed* it. Needed her to forget everything but me and how I made her feel.

"Please," she said. "I want it. I..." I brought her to the edge again, drinking in her helpless cries: "More... Please... I need it. I need you."

"That's right, you do. I'm the only one you need. Remember your promise? I'm the only man who touches you. The only man that fucking *looks* at you."

"I know, I know. I promised...only you."

"Damn right, you did."

But I still wasn't satisfied. I brought her to the edge one more time and held her there.

When her voice was raw from pleading, I rolled on the condom and, lifting her legs, pulled her to the end of the mattress and drove into her, my focus on where we were joined.

"Watch us," I told her. "Watch me taking you."

She lifted her head and complied. "Sweet Luna," she said, her tits bouncing with each thrust. "That's...hot."

When I glanced up, she eyed me, heavy-lidded, her face a mask of lust. I angled my hips and slowed my strokes, making contact with her clit with each plunge inside her.

"That's right, baby. Look at the man whose gonna make you come."

"Yes." She swiveled her pelvis, making me groan in response. "Yesyesyes... Please, Spider."

"*Now.*" I slid my thumb between our bodies, massaging her swollen little bud until she broke, hips jerking, my name on her lips.

She was still spasming around me when I gripped her knees and pushed them even wider so I could get that extra fraction of an inch inside her. "Take me, pretty Lark. Take all of me."

Burying my face in her throat, I scraped my teeth over her skin without breaking it, my fangs literally aching to sink into her. But the protective part of me, which she'd somehow triggered, put the brakes on. I'd already fed from her the other night, and she'd been hurt, and healing takes energy. She needed another night or so to recover.

"More." Lark's hands came to my hips, her nails digging into my ass. "Harder."

Lifting my head, I gave the lady what she was begging for, pounding into her until my release tore through me like an out-of-control train. Beneath me, she was coming again, too, sobbing out, "Spider, Spider, Spider," like I was some kinda sex god.

Which was how she made me feel, and damn, it was

addictive.

She was addictive.

A helpless sound rasped from the depths of my being. I stilled, emptying myself into her, my dick jerking, greedily taking more pleasure until I felt squeezed dry and more satisfied than I could ever recall being.

I hung over Lark's body, struggling for breath.

She stroked my lower back. "Mm. I like your style, Spider-Man."

I grunted, incapable of forming even a single word, and nuzzling her beneath her ear, settled my full weight on her.

Not wanting to move.

Not wanting to let her go.

Amina wormed her way into my brain. I closed my eyes, trying to shut her out, until Lark straightened her legs, reminding I outweighed her by at least sixty pounds. I crawled off her, waiting as she scooted fully onto the bed before flopping onto my back beside her.

I stared at the ceiling, bracing myself for the guilt to crash in like an unwanted guest. And it did, but not as forcefully as usual. This was more like the habit of guilt, something I felt because I thought I should, especially after enjoying the hell out of another woman.

Lark rolled onto her side and traced a finger down my nose and over my lips. "What're you thinking?"

That edge of yearning was back in her voice. I didn't need to look to know it was written all over her face.

This is where I should push her away. Remind her she was only a body to me.

But she was opening up to me, and I liked that. I *wanted* Lark to talk to me freely, to feel safe with me.

She started to withdraw, bringing her hand to the mattress between us, and my gut clenched. Rejecting her felt wrong.

I wasn't sure what she was to me—or what she could become. All I knew was that I wanted to know her better.

"You." I turned my head, meeting her eyes. "I'm thinking about you."

She gulped, a mix of surprise and vulnerability flashing across her face. My slow-beating heart gave a single hard thump, the weight of my words hanging in the air.

But I didn't take them back.

8

———————

LARK

My belly fluttered.

That was the last thing I'd expected Spider to say. I'd figured he'd turn his head and say he had to get going. Or that he was up for another round.

"I'm thinking about you."

And it wasn't just the words, it was the way he'd said it, kind of...tenderly. Like thinking about me made him happy.

"Lark?" he asked, his eyes crinkling at the edges, and I realized I was staring at him, mouth ajar.

I snapped my mouth closed and turned my head because I couldn't *think*. He made me stupid.

What was his deal, anyway?

When he'd caught me playing pools with the guys, he'd gone all alpha vampire on me. Monster had taken one look at his face and backed away, muttering, "Uh-oh."

Uneasiness had tripped up my spine, but I'd lined up my next shot like I couldn't feel Spider's eyes boring into me. So what if he was king down here and so far dominant to me, we weren't even in the same building, let alone on the same level?

I would *not* be intimidated. I was his thrall, not his blood slave.

But he didn't seem to care I made some money off his people so long as I played fair. And I had—played fair, that is. I mean, I could've cheated, but where was the fun in that? Somewhere on the other side, Mom and Dad were shaking their heads, muttering I'd gone soft. But I liked Spider's people. They'd been nice to me, damn it.

And now here Spider was, eyeing me like I was the most interesting person in the world. He'd even invited me to join his lair.

I could not figure him out, and it made me edgy, and yet, I also...wanted.

He rolled onto his side and brushed my hair back from my temple. "What's goin' on in that mind of yours?"

My throat clogged. I felt bashful, like a thirteen-year-old around her first crush.

Me. The woman who'd never met a man she couldn't handle.

But I wasn't used to this degree of attention—not when I was being myself. When I was playing a part, sure. But not when I was *Lark*.

Even Troll hadn't looked at me like that. He'd only wanted my body. Spider stared at me like he was trying to see into my brain.

I had to force myself not to squirm on the mattress.

Deflect, deflect.

It was instinct to hide myself. That's what I'd been taught, and the reason I'd survived the past six months.

Instead, I heard myself ask, all breathy and feminine, "Thinking about me how?"

He propped his head on his hand, hard-muscled and beautiful. The man could cut glass with those biceps. "For one thing, I'm wondering how you ended up with Grimclaw."

Oh. So this was about Grim. Inside, the hopeful, excited fluttering wobbled to a halt.

"He's my cousin."

"I know. But you had nowhere else to go?"

"Sad, huh?" I made a comic face to hide the fact that it *was* sad.

He didn't smile. "Yeah. The man isn't fit to be alpha of himself, let alone a lair."

I turned my head so I was looking up at the ceiling. "I know that now. But I didn't have a lot of choices, you know?"

"Because he wasn't affiliated with a syndicate?"

Yes. But that was too close to the truth, so I prevaricated. "Why would that matter?"

"You don't belong down here—anyone can see that. People like you, they're usually on the run from some syndicate."

I made a noncommittal sound.

Even Grimclaw didn't know Jared Darkman was hunting me. He knew I'd had to leave Nevada in a hurry, but he thought it was a heist gone wrong. The story fit what he knew about me and my parents.

The truth? My parents tried to con the spoiled heir of the Las Vegas primus.

Jared had staked them. Me? He had a different fate in mind.

I swallowed noisily.

"Lark?" Spider touched my cheek. "What aren't you telling me?"

I tensed, my instincts screaming a warning.

Time to shut this down.

I couldn't trust anyone. I couldn't involve anyone.

Good sex—even if it had been earth-shattering, brain-melting sex—didn't mean tossing my caution out the window.

I lifted a brow. "Excuse me, but why is this your business?"

"Hey." He picked up my hand and kissed it. Without my meaning to, my fingers closed on his like a lifeline. "I don't give two fucks who you're hiding from, but if you want me to give someone a beatdown, just say the word."

I blinked rapidly. *Damn*. Way to hit me in the feels.

I'd been on my own for so long. Grimclaw didn't count; I only trusted him so far.

"Who says I'm hiding from anyone?"

Spider sighed. "Lark…"

I grimaced. "Sorry."

He waited, and somehow, I found myself telling him more. He needed to know. In case Jared Darkman found me. Or if I suddenly disappeared…

"Fine. You're right. I *am* hiding from someone—and that's all I'm going to say."

"Oh, baby." He gathered me in his arms.

I snuggled into what was rapidly becoming my safe place, my nose in the spot between his neck and shoulder.

A big, powerful hand stroked my back. "You know I'm on your side, right? Somebody tries to fuck with you, they're gonna have to go through me first."

"Sure."

I didn't believe him, but I appreciated that he'd said it. But when Jared Darkman finally caught up to me, the Vegas Syndicate would bring a world of pain down on Spider if he tried to help me.

He shook my shoulder. "Dammit, Lark. I mean it."

I rubbed my cheek against his dark stubble, taking his scent onto my skin like a cat. Something to remember in the years to come when this month with him was in the rearview mirror. "Drop it. Please?"

His chest heaved but he fell silent.

I rolled my lips into my mouth. Time to lighten things up.

Pulling out of his arms, I rolled onto my side, head on my palm. "Now I've got a question for you."

"Anything," he answered.

"What's green, fuzzy, and would hurt if it fell on you out of a tree?"

His thick brows drew together in confusion. "I dunno. What?"

I grinned, even though it wasn't that funny and I felt anything but happy. "A pool table."

He blinked, then gave a reluctant smile. "Hah. Now I have a question for you—three questions, actually."

I eyed him warily. "Yeah?"

"I wanna know three things about you. Not something that's a secret," he added when I started to shake my head. "Start with your favorite dessert."

"Oh." I relaxed. "Then I'm gonna go with a classic—chocolate chip cookies. Right after they come out of the oven, all warm and gooey."

His mouth curved. "That was my go-to when I was a little dude. My mama made the best cookies in Brooklyn."

"She's gone now?"

"Yeah, she passed a few years ago."

"I'm sorry."

He dipped his chin in acknowledgment. "She wasn't happy when I was turned, especially because I did it partly for her— so I could buy her a nice house, send her on a trip to Hawaii. She was a teacher, but she got hurt and had to go out on disability, and she had no savings. And she always wanted to see Hawaii."

"Did she go?"

"Yep." His expression warmed, his love for his mom clear. "Took me a couple of years to get the cash together, and then another year to convince her to take it. But she did."

I tried and failed to picture anyone refusing Spider for over a year. "Yeah? She sounds like some woman."

"She was. I miss her every day."

"I'm sorry," I said softly.

He heaved a breath. "She wouldn't let me turn her. Said she didn't wanna live that long. Anyway. What tunes get you hyped?"

"That's easy—anything I can dance to. But hip-hop's my go-to."

"Same," he said. "And salsa."

"Salsa, huh? Bet you have some good moves."

"You bet your sweet ass I do."

"Modest, too."

His eyes creased at the corners, and in my chest, a dozen butterflies flapped crazily. I couldn't tell if I was happy or scared, but maybe that was because it was both.

"Last question," he said. "Where *did* you learn to play pool like that? Monster and Jacko don't lose to many people."

"I told you, I was home-schooled. Dad wanted me to have a skill I could fall back on if I needed to, and Mom was all about the geometry and physics applications."

"Huh." He eyed me. "They sound pretty interesting."

Grief twisted through me. But beneath the sorrow, anger simmered.

"They were," I said, throat tight.

"So they're gone?"

"Yeah." Before he could ask more, I said, "That's three— now it's my turn. If you could go anywhere in the world, where would you go?"

"Nowhere," he replied promptly. "I'm right where I want to be."

"Oh, you're good at this."

He touched my face. "I mean it."

His deep-brown eyes had warmed, his expression soft, open...as if he really, really liked me. The room around us faded, the sounds in the Cavern outside muted. It was just us, wrapped in a cocoon of wordless understanding.

Inside me, those butterflies took flight. A burst of longing hit me, so hard my heart actually hurt.

I couldn't stay with him for much longer. It was too risky.

I'd already stayed in New York for longer than I should've. Frankly, I was surprised I'd evaded Jared this long, but my gamble had paid off—he must've figured I'd never go to ground in the Underworld. The classy syndicate lady I'd pretended to be wouldn't have survived down here a week.

"Maybe," I said, "I could hang around another month. If that's okay?"

"Of course." Spider cupped my cheek, and I got the feeling he heard more than what I'd said. "But if you change your mind about joining my lair permanently, the offer stands."

I turned my head, pressing my lips to his callused palm, wishing with all my heart I could take him up on his offer. But it was only a matter of time before Jared found me, and the longer I stayed in one place, the easier I made it for him.

So all I said was, "Thank you."

9

SPIDER

Three nights later, I dropped out of the shadows near Grimclaw's lair and stared down at a thin, neatly made mattress crammed into a rough, six-by-ten-feet burrow. Five plastic crates stacked in a pyramid formed a makeshift headboard.

This was where Lark had been sleeping? I'd seen larger jail cells.

She wasn't even in Grimclaw's main lair. She was in this side spur, almost completely unprotected. Yeah, the entrance to her "bedroom"—or whatever you'd call it—was through a small opening behind a rock-filled garbage can, but if I'd been able to track her to the burrow, then other supernaturals could.

I eyed the crates, which along with serving as her headboard, were also filled with clothes. When I'd decided to surprise Lark by retrieving her things, I hadn't thought it would be so fucking easy—or that she'd own so little.

Anger surged through me. How could Grimclaw be so reckless with her? I clenched my fists, wanting to smash something, preferably the ass's face.

My jaw hardened. One way or another, Lark's cousin was going down.

I crouched down and unzipped the duffel bag I'd brought. A couple of rats popped out of one of the crates, watching, bright-eyed, as I stuffed Lark's clothes into it.

A half-dozen tees. White sneakers and a pair of red patent-leather ankle boots. Leggings and a couple pairs of pants. The top crate held two rolled-up dresses—a green stretchy-thing and something in a shimmery gold material. I laid her black leather jacket on top and added the nylon backpack I found next to the crates stuffed with her underwear and socks.

Before leaving, I did a quick sweep of the tiny space in case I'd missed something valuable—money, jewelry, a weapon. I even checked under the mattress.

I found zip. Lark's entire life fit into a single duffel bag.

My brows drew together. Something didn't add up.

The woman was a kickass thief. I should know.

Not to mention her side gig as a pool shark.

So why was she living like a goddamn Cinderella? Was Grimclaw forcing her to give every penny she made—and if so, why had she allowed it? Was his protection that important to her?

I zipped up the duffel bag and slung it over my shoulder before ducking out of the narrow exit. The last thing I did was pick up the rock-filled trash can and heave it at the lair's entrance. It smashed into the thick wood door with a satisfying thud, the rocks tumbling out.

For good measure, I bared my fangs at the camera trained on the tunnel, daring him to come out and say something. But either Grimclaw wasn't home or he didn't have the balls to confront me. He'd know I'd declared war on him, though. I left the rocks where they'd fallen, blocking the entrance, and headed back to the Cavern at a jog.

What was Lark's deal, anyway? You'd think she'd jump at

the chance to join my lair. Instead, all she'd given me was a measly extra month.

It's not like she had it so good in her cousin's lair. Did she really prefer those assholes to me?

But as I covered the miles between my lair and Grimclaw's, I had to face the truth: Lark's reluctance was on me. I'd thought I was so smart, blackmailing her into becoming my thrall.

I'd get to fuck her, and when the month was over, I'd pay her off and send her on her way. No mess, no drama, right?

Wrong.

I would *never* be okay with Lark leaving, and now she was rightfully wary of me. Like you would be with a man who'd informed you that he owned you.

As for me, I was fascinated by her, hoarding details about her like a dragon and his gold. Her favorite cookie. The way she liked things neat and orderly. The long, hot showers she took each night to help her "wake up."

Those ridiculous jokes she made.

Her laugh. The way it bubbled out of her, low and happy...

Hell, my entire lair had fallen under her spell. They didn't even mind her hustling them in pool because she'd started dropping some tips in return.

Even DeeDee, the toughest nut to crack, had warmed up to her. The twenty-something human was hella protective of me. Not because we had a thing (other than the occasional feed-and-fuck), but because she'd been living on the streets when Velma had found her and offered her a place in the Cavern. DeeDee still didn't trust I wouldn't change my mind and boot her out.

I turned a corner, and as if I'd conjured her with my thoughts, there was DeeDee. "Spider!" She startled, hunching her bony shoulders like she expected me to hit her. "I-I was just out for a walk."

She darted a frightened look from beneath her straight

black bangs. I frowned. Her skittishness around me was annoying, but she was Velma's project, not mine.

"Yeah? Well, next time take a friend, alright? The other lairs know you belong to the Cavern, but the Underworld's a big place. There are vampires down here—lone wolves—that no one ever sees." And those vampires were hungry, but DeeDee ought to know that by now.

She blinked rapidly. "Sorry, sir. I won't do it again. I was on my way back, anyway."

"Walk with me," I invited.

She gulped, but fell in with me. I slowed my pace to accommodate her. A human couldn't navigate the uneven terrain of cracked concrete and bent tracks at my speed.

"So how are things?" I asked.

A wary look. "What d'you mean?"

"You've been with us what—six months, now? You're settling in?"

"Yeah, absolutely. Everyone's been good to me. And everything's going great. Just great."

"Okay." I slanted her a look, wondering why her enthusiasm seemed forced. "You'd tell me if there was a problem, right? Or Velma."

"I would, yeah." She nodded several times.

We reached the lair door. I entered the combination and waved a hand for her to enter before me.

DeeDee hesitated, biting her lip.

"What?" I asked.

"I just wanna say thanks—for everything. I feel like I should be paying you something. I've got some money saved from my bartending gig and—"

"Keep it," I interrupted. "And you do contribute. You cook and clean, and we can always use an extra human to feed from. So as far as I'm concerned, we're good."

"Right. Sure." Ducking her head, she hurried into the Cavern, veering off toward the passage that led to her bedroom.

I watched her go, my brows knitted together, then shrugged. I wasn't a goddamn counselor.

I caught sight of Lark, laughing on the couch with Zayne, and forgot all about DeeDee. I strode toward her, pulled by an invisible magnet, barely noticing the people between us until Bliss stopped me with a question. I bit back a sigh and heard her out because, with both of her parents gone, the blue-haired teenager had glommed on to me as a father figure. But after I dealt with her, I went straight to Lark.

10

LARK

Spider stalked into the lair, his lean, athletic form in a black T-shirt and Army-green tactical pants, and zeroed in on me.

I straightened and ran a hand down my hair, forgetting what I'd been about to say to Zayne, who was lounging on the couch beside me.

Zayne followed my gaze. "He always knows exactly where you are, doesn't he?"

"You think?"

"You haven't noticed?"

I shrugged, my gaze glued to his as he headed in my direction, jaw set, oblivious to the people edging out of his way. Until Bliss stopped him. Then he set down the duffel bag in his hand so he could put an arm around her, giving her his entire focus until she was done. He squeezed her shoulders and slipped her some cash, and I felt a little piece of my heart break off and fall at his feet.

The hard-ass kingpin had a soft spot for Bliss, the weakest member of his crew other than DeeDee. I respected the hell out of him for that.

But damn, he was making it hard for me to keep my distance.

Bliss gave him a shy hug back, then took off, and Spider continued to me. He had that set look about him again, like he was pissed off about something.

"This is for you." He dropped the duffel bag at my feet like a big cat showing off its prey.

I blinked up at him, feeling kinda raw. "For me?"

"Yeah. Open it."

"Ooh," Zayne murmured. "A surprise."

Spider's gaze flicked to her. "Don't you have somewhere to be?"

"And miss the show?" she returned. "Besides, this is my night off."

I froze, still half-expecting Spider to backhand a low-ranking soldier like Zayne for mouthing off to him, especially when he was already angry about something.

But he just jerked his chin at me. "Open it, already."

Everyone in the Cavern had turned to watch. I pulled the bag closer.

Had he—?

I unzipped the bag. The first thing I saw was my backpack, the one I'd picked up at a thrift shop on my way out of Vegas, with my leather jacket beneath it.

He had.

My gaze snapped to Spider. "You got my things?"

"Figured you'd want your own clothes and shit. So you don't have to go back to Grimclaw for anything. And just so you know, I told him he's not your alpha anymore—I am." He crossed his arms over his chest, daring me to object.

I drew a breath, aware of everyone listening to our exchange. It was a high-handed, very alpha thing to do, but that was Spider. I should point out that he had no right to do that, but my relief was too strong. I wouldn't have to see Grim again. Even better, I'd never have to see Troll again.

"Thank you," I said gratefully.

Spider shrugged a shoulder and seemed to settle, the aggression easing. "No problem."

I set the backpack aside and pulled out the leather jacket. Zayne ran a hand over the buttery soft leather. "Niiiice. What else d'you have in there?"

I barely heard her, my eyes locked on the Rabanne dress shimmering up at me. Even on Net-a-Porter, the Rabanne had cost more than the rest of my clothes combined. Mom had bought it when we hit Las Vegas. It was the last thing she ever got me.

My vision blurred. I smashed my lips together, fighting back tears.

I put the leather jacket on the couch and carefully lifted out the sleeveless gold dress.

"Damn," said Zayne. "That's fire. Bet you look hot in it, too."

I held it to my chest and mouthed another heartfelt "Thank you," at Spider, who gave me a crooked smile in return.

I placed the dress on my lap and rifled through the rest of the bag. It was all there. He'd even brought my shoes.

Spider unfolded his arms. "That's everything, right? Unless you had something inside Grimclaw's lair?"

"No. This is it."

Zayne ran a hand over her short red hair. "You weren't inside Grimclaw's lair? Aren't you the dude's cousin?"

"It's complicated," I told her.

His mouth compressed. That's when it hit me that he'd seen my make-shift den, knew that I'd been sleeping outside Grimclaw's lair. Was that what had pissed him off? And he wasn't just angry. That vertical crease between his brows told me he had questions. Questions I didn't want to answer.

"You should take her clubbing," Zayne told Spider. "In that dress."

His eyes warmed. "I should."

I stiffened in alarm. "No! I mean, that's okay. Really."

The last time Jared saw me, I'd been wearing the gold dress. I didn't dare appear in it again, even this far from Darkman territory. And I definitely didn't want to draw attention by going clubbing with the notorious Spider, the mysterious New York Underworld kingpin. Show up on his arm, and everyone would wonder who I was. Before I knew it, we'd be on someone's Instagram.

Zayne and Spider turned identical frowns on me.

"Why not?" he asked.

I fingered the Rabanne's silky gold material and muttered, "I'm not much of a dancer."

That was a lie. I loved dressing up and going out to nightclubs. It was one of the best things about my old life, playing the princess—that is, a high-ranking vampire syndicate member—while my parents and I scoped out the best way to swipe whatever jewels or art we were after.

"Really," Spider said flatly. "You told me your favorite tunes were anything you can dance to."

Gods, I hated lying to him even about something this small. But I was committed now.

"I did, but—" I screwed up my nose. "No rhythm."

Zayne's brows climbed. "But the other night, when Jacko put on 'In Da Club,' you were shaking it with the rest of us."

I blew out a breath. "Can we just drop it? I don't wanna go, okay?"

"Sure," she said, although I could tell she didn't understand.

I rolled up the dress, avoiding both her and Spider's eyes.

Maybe it was because I'd already been feeling raw and a little vulnerable, but this bomb of warmth had detonated in my belly and I had no clue how to handle it. Spider really did want me in his lair. This—getting my clothes—was proof. He wanted to demonstrate that I didn't have to go back to Grimclaw for anything.

And here I was lying to him again. Even if it wasn't a big deal—I mean who cared whether I could dance?—it made me feel dirty.

"I'll just go put these things away." I reached for the duffel bag but Spider got to it first.

"I'll bring it."

"Thanks." I scooped up the rest, still avoiding his eyes, and hurried toward our bedroom.

No, Lark. Not our *bedroom. His* bedroom.

As soon as the door shut behind us, Spider said, "Is everything cool? You wanted your things, right?"

"Of course, I did. Just let me..." Even with this emotion-bomb tearing up my insides, I couldn't thank Spider properly until the Rabanne was safely on a hanger in his closet.

I slid the dress onto a hanger and hung it next to one of Spider's silk shirts, my mind flashing back to the last time I'd worn it, and how much I missed Mom and Dad.

Because I did. Every single day.

Even after what they'd done to me, I missed them.

But laid on top of that was this...wanting.

I wanted to go out clubbing—on Spider's arm. Wanted the whole world to know we were a couple. Just...wanted.

Grimclaw had only begrudgingly given me sanctuary. If he'd known how dangerous it was to hide me, he would've tossed me out on my ass.

Spider wouldn't do that.

Spider was the kind of guy who'd protect his own, and for some reason, he'd decided I was his. If I told him the truth, he'd try to help me. Starting with going after that prick Jared.

And I couldn't let that happen. Jared and his primus father were too powerful. They'd stomp Spider and Zayne and

Monster and the rest into the concrete with their fancy Italian-leather boots—and laugh while doing it.

As alpha, Spider *couldn't* choose me—and I couldn't let him. He had his lair to protect.

I hung the leather jacket on a peg, but before I could return to the bedroom, Spider spoke from behind me, his voice deep and a little rough. "Lark?"

A hot shiver went over my skin. "What?" I asked without turning around.

His hands closed on my shoulders. "Would you wear that dress for me?" he asked against the side of my neck.

"Tonight?"

"No. I mean out. To the Midnight Masquerade."

Oh, gods. He was gutting me here.

The Kral's Midnight Masquerade was a big freaking deal in the vampire world. The Kral Syndicate—the syndicate who ruled most of the East Coast from New York on south—didn't let just anyone come, either.

"You have an invite?" I stalled.

"Mm-hm." He nuzzled my ear. "You know the Kral brothers?"

"Yeah. I mean, I haven't met them, but I know *of* them." The Dark Angels, as the three brothers were known, were famous in both the human and vampire worlds. The fact that all three were serious eye-candy didn't hurt.

"The middle brother is a friend of mine—Zaq."

"What?" I craned my neck to look at him. "You serious?"

"I did him a favor a couple of years back, and now he has his dad paying me to police the Underworld." Spider smirked. "Easiest money I ever made."

"That must've been some favor."

"It was. Saved the dude's ass—he would've been pushing up daisies without my help, and he made sure Karoly knew it. Plus,

Zaq hires us as backup security when he needs a couple of extra men."

I blinked. Spider and Zaq must be really, really good friends because I'd never heard of a syndicate prince hiring Underworld people as security.

"Zaq's okay for a rich mofo," Spider added. "You'd like him and his mate. She's some long-lost syndicate princess, but she didn't grow up rich like he did. Woman's a certified badass."

His affection for Zaq and his mate came through in his voice. I found myself wanting to go to the Midnight Masquerade just to see Spider in that world. I'd wager he was pretty badass himself, as in *I'm the coolest dude here and I don't even have to try.*

"So?" He skated his lips down the side of my neck. "Wanna come to the Masquerade with me? And don't give me that you-don't-dance crap." He slapped my ass. "I told you what happens if you lie to me."

"Sorry." I pouted, but underneath, I didn't mind that he'd called me on the untruth.

"So you'll come?"

"I—"

Red flags were waving like a parade of danger signs. For one thing, I needed to pull back from Spider, pull back from this wanting. And two, there was my Jared Darkman problem.

Spider turned me around. Now I had to meet his eyes, the deep, chocolatey brown sucking me in.

"What?" he asked. "Tell me."

"I'm sorry, but—" My gaze slid from his. "I just can't, okay?"

11

SPIDER

An hour later, I rolled off Lark. She cuddled up to me, a hand on my chest.

Now that the edge was off, I couldn't get the conditions that she'd been living in out of my mind. Toying with her hair—the same hair I'd pulled as she'd screamed out her last climax—I asked, "You think any more about staying permanently?"

She pulled away. "I don't think so, ya know? But thanks for the offer."

The side of my body where she'd been curled up felt cold. I turned to face her. "You're not going back to Grimclaw's lair."

"You telling me or asking me?"

Sweet Lord, I was tired of her evasions. The woman was more slippery than a fish. "Yes or no," I snapped.

"Fine. Then no, I'm not going back."

"Then why not stay with us? I'd take care of you. You have my oath on it."

"Yeah?" The naked yearning on her face made my chest compress.

This woman would want all of me. But I didn't have all of me to give, did I?

I flashed on the pile of ash and charred bones that had been all that was left of Amina when I'd finally tracked her down. And like a yellow-belly, I backpedaled, pretending I hadn't meant anything other than an offer to join my lair.

"Sure. We're family here. I take care of everyone in the Cavern."

"I've seen that. They're lucky."

"Your alpha out West wasn't like that?"

"I never had a real alpha. Grimclaw was the first."

"Him?" I curled my lip. "He's a goddamn cartoon alpha. I'm surprised he's lasted as long as he has. But how did you survive without an alpha?"

A shrug. "My parents were good at surviving."

"We're talking about California?"

She hesitated, and I wondered why I kept pressing her, why I couldn't let her keep her secrets like everyone else in the Cavern.

"Not just California," she said. "Arizona. Nevada. Washington State for a while. We kept moving."

I knew that from the check we'd run on her, but now I wanted to know why her parents had been taken out—and who the fuck was responsible. "What happened six months ago?"

She didn't move or even tense up, but I *felt* her withdraw like she'd slammed a metal barricade between us. "You know about that, huh?"

"Not really. All we could dig up was that three of you dropped off the grid around then."

"Yeah. Well, what happened was they did something stupid." Grief washed over her features. "So, so stupid."

My stomach churned. I was starting to understand why a woman like Lark was hiding in the Underworld. I planked myself over her, my forearms on either side of her head. "So Grimclaw's all you have?"

She snorted. "No. *I'm* all I have."

I frowned. She was a dhampir in the Wild West of the Underworld. I didn't like the idea of her being out there without protection.

"Stay with me, Lark. You go out there without an alpha at your back, and another vampire will snatch you up, make you a blood slave. You don't have the same rights as a human. Everyone would look the other way."

She swallowed and briefly closed her eyes. When she opened them again, she said, "Just let them try. I'll drive a stake into my own heart before I let someone make me a slave."

I ground my back teeth together. Why was she being so damn stubborn? "I could make you stay."

She speared me with a look and I knew we were both recalling my promise to let her go after thirty days. But instead of throwing it in my face, she arched up, rubbing her wet pussy against my erection. "Yeah? How?"

"Cut the shit. Distracting me won't work." But my hips rocked against hers, my dick not caring that she was playing me. It just wanted back inside her hot, tight channel.

"Is that what I'm doing?" she asked, all wide-eyed and pouty. The woman should've gone to Hollywood—she could do innocence like an A-lister. "I thought I was being a good, obedient thrall. One who's on a *thirty-day contract*, remember?"

And there it was. My jaw worked.

Fucking agreement.

"I remember," I admitted.

"Just making sure." Her breasts heaved, the tips brushing over the hair on my chest. "Look, I'm fine, alright? Leave it in the past where it belongs. You'll just kick up a hornet's nest."

Hornet's nest?

My whole body tensed. "Tell me you weren't part of this 'stupid' thing your parents did."

She met my eyes. "If I was, d'you think I'd be here, talking to you? But to be clear—no, I wasn't." Her lips thinned. "That was all them."

I studied her, certain she was holding something back. But I also understood she thought her only choice was to prevaricate. Whatever had happened, it had scarred her, and living with Grimclaw had just made things worse.

"You sure? Because I have a rep, you know. Gimme the names and I'll tell them to leave you the fuck alone. And if they don't, I'll make them sorry."

She blinked a couple of times. "You'd do that? Even when I'm not officially a member of your lair?"

"Join my lair and that's not an issue. Because if you're in trouble, I can help. You just have to trust me."

She worried her lower lip with her teeth, and I thought I'd gotten through to her. Then she stretched her mouth into a fake smile, the kind that didn't touch her eyes.

"I appreciate the offer, but staying isn't my style, alright? People like me and my parents, we keep moving."

"Bullshit. You're afraid."

"Oh, so now you're in my brain? You know what, get off me." She pushed at my chest, trying to slither out from under me.

I shoved my disappointment down deep. The woman didn't want to stay, fine.

Spider didn't beg.

Why are you pressuring her like this, anyway? You can't keep her. She'd be a weakness, a way to get to you...like Amina.

But it made me a little crazy to think Lark might be in danger and was refusing to ask for help. The anger I'd felt when I'd seen that hole in the wall she'd called home reared its head again.

"Settle down." I lowered my body, pinning her to the mattress. "You don't wanna tell me, that's your prerogative."

She eyed me, making sure I meant it, before relaxing back onto the mattress.

"Now, open your legs," I told her.

"Again?" she asked.

I arched a brow. "Did that sound like a question?"

Her breath hitched. Slowly, her knees bent until her thighs hugged my hips.

"Keep them like that," I ordered, grabbing a condom and rolling it on.

I nudged my dick up against her opening. She was still wet and swollen from the last time, which was good, because I wasn't in the mood for foreplay. I wanted to be inside her, showing her who her master was. Using her like I'd paid twenty-five grand for.

I extended my fangs, sinking them into her at the same time I thrust deep inside her snug pussy. She gasped, and a part of me enjoyed it, the part that wanted to dominate her, extract every last fucking secret from her.

A better man might've apologized, but I wasn't sorry. Being inside her in this way, my mouth filled with the taste of her, felt too good.

I drank greedily, and thrust again. Taking what I wanted because this at least, I could control.

Except Lark didn't seem to mind. Instead, she wrapped her arms and legs around me, her body straining toward mine, trying to take me deeper.

"Harder," she rasped against my ear.

Slay. Me.

I groaned against her soft skin and gave it to her harder.

12

LARK

Spider licked the wounds he'd made in my neck closed and withdrew from me, rolling onto his back. The room was silent except for our pounding hearts.

I felt him eyeing me. I braced myself for more questions, but instead, he picked up my hand and kissed it, then rose from the bed with that easy grace he had. A few seconds later, the shower came on.

I sat up in his bed, covers pulled to my chest.

A shudder went over me. I'd been so close to giving into him, telling him the whole story and naming Jared Darkman as the reason I was in hiding.

Dammit, Lark. He's getting to you.

He made me want things, and I couldn't let that happen.

My gaze settled on the duffel bag. Why had he gone and done such a nice thing? He was confusing me, dammit. I could take whatever he threw at me in bed. Hell, I loved it.

But this was starting to feel like more—a relationship. Which he didn't want any more than me, right?

But I do. I do want it.

I dropped my head into my hands and dug my palms into my eyes.

You're so fucked, Lark.

I drew a breath, then threw off the covers and went into the bathroom. Spider had pulled his locks into a high man-bun to keep them dry and was soaping his underarms. His head snapped up, tracking my movements as I put my own hair up in a ponytail and stepped into the shower, closing the door behind me.

Hot water rained around us. He rubbed the soap over the taut ridges and grooves of his abs, giving me a lazy smile. My gaze tracked a stream of tiny bubbles, following their path down the deep cut bisecting his lower torso to where they disappeared into the black nest of hair around his rapidly hardening dick. He returned the soap to its holder and circled his soapy fingers around himself, running them to the tip and back to the root in a leisurely squeeze.

With an effort, I brought my gaze back to his face. His brown eyes were hot and knowing, but I sensed a barrier between us, a barrier that was as much my fault as his.

This thing between us had to end. It wasn't safe for either of us for me to stay too long—that hadn't changed.

And Spider wasn't offering me forever anyway. If Amina had truly been his mate, then he never would.

I swallowed what felt like shards of glass. If only I'd met him first...

But before I left, I wanted that night out with Spider that he'd dangled before me like a glittering necklace. One special night with my gorgeous, badass Underworld kingpin.

Yeah, Jared was an issue, but the syndicates tended to stick to their own except for strategic alliances, and the Darkmans and the Krals had never entered into an alliance.

Plus, it's the Midnight Masquerade, *dammit.*

I wanted to go with him so bad, and a masquerade meant

masks, right? I'd just have to make sure mine stayed on. Jared would be looking for a blonde, and I'd gone back to my natural black the night after I left Vegas.

"I'll go," I said, moving closer.

He stopped stroking himself and lifted an eyebrow. "To the Masquerade?"

I put a hand on his arm, breathing in his clean, male scent. My heart turned over at how familiar that smell had become— the hint of coconut, the maleness of it.

"Yes. If the invite still stands, that is."

His brows drew together. I *felt* his questions, pressing against my skin. But all he said was, "All right."

I rose on my toes, and taking his face in my hands, kissed him. One deep, soul-kiss, pouring everything I couldn't say, even to myself, into it.

He stiffened, then brought a hand to my ass, urging me against him. But when I dropped back to my heels, he let me go.

I reached for the soap and started to wash myself. "I need a new dress, though."

"What's the matter with the gold dress?"

"I can't wear it." Not after I'd worn it to a party at the Darkman's over-the-top Vegas mansion.

Spider was frowning now, so I added, "Too many memories," which was also true. "My mom bought it for me. I was wearing it the night they..." I rolled my lips in and shrugged.

Spider wrapped a long arm around me, pulling me to him. "Hey, it's okay. I'll buy you a new dress, okay, baby?"

Baby. I bit my lip, knowing that meant he wasn't angry at me anymore.

And despite everything I'd told myself, that emotion-bomb went off in me again. This time it was more like an expanding balloon, lifting me in its wake.

"I can buy it for myself," I said. "That wasn't a hint." I'd amassed a decent amount of cash playing pool with his crew, although sometimes I suspected Monster, at least, was letting me win because he'd guessed how much I needed the money.

Spider touched his forehead to mine. "I wanna do it, okay? A gift."

"Yeah?" My smile came from deep inside. "Then, alright. And thank you. When is the Masquerade, anyway?"

"November twenty-ninth. And Lark?" He caught my lower lip between his teeth, then released it. "If I buy the dress, I get to pick it out."

My inner thighs squeezed together at the way he said it. Half-promise, half-threat.

I slid my hands up his chest, teasing his nipples with my thumbs. "Should I be worried?"

"Probably," he said against my mouth. "But you're gonna let me do it anyway."

13

SPIDER

Sometimes I had really bad ideas. I mean, really fucking terrible ideas.

Like taking Lark dress shopping.

It was the following Monday, and we were at some fancy little shop in Soho. I'd instructed the saleswoman to find us a dress for the Midnight Masquerade, then parked myself on a spindly chair in the pink-and-black dressing room, a glass of blood-whiskey in hand, to give the thumbs-up or thumbs-down on the choices.

Now I was being tortured by Lark in a series of cock-teasing dresses. A short white lacy thing that was so see-through you could tell the color of her nipples. A longer red dress with a back that dipped so low you could see the top of her ass cheeks.

I took a sip of blood-whiskey and shrugged off my leather jacket, undoing the first two buttons of my silk shirt for good measure. Why did humans keep their buildings so damn hot?

The saleswoman glanced at me and I shook my head, nixing the red like I had the white-lace dress. She helped Lark remove it, leaving her barefoot on the thick pink carpet in a black thong and no bra. Anything else would "spoil the lines," the saleswoman had informed us.

Next up was a slinky silver tube that bared Lark's buttercream throat and shoulders. "No," I barked before she even got a chance to see herself in the dressing room's trio of mirrors. "Find something that doesn't show so much of her neck."

The Midnight Masquerade was a playground for vampires at their most decadent. Taking Lark dressed like that would be like dangling a piece of raw meat in front of a pack of starving wolves, and I'd rather not get in a brawl over her at a syndicate ball. Not that I feared those arrogant SOBs, but I preferred to fly under the radar.

"Of course, sir." The saleswoman peeled Lark out of the silver tube.

I waited until she was putting yet another dress on Lark and adjusted my dick. The saleswoman didn't see, but Lark pressed her lips together, trying not to laugh.

I glowered back at her.

The current choice was a deep, purply red with a high neck that encircled Lark's throat like a collar. A diamond cutout dipped between her breasts, and another, smaller diamond opened over her mid-back. At her hips, the dress flared into a short, pleated skirt over a black gauze slip. The slip was tighter and designed to peek beneath the skirt, an edgy touch that was perfect for Lark.

"Do a little shimmy," said the saleswoman, and when Lark complied, the pleats changed from red to purple and back again.

Lark's eyes widened. She shook her hips again. "Wow. That's so freaking cool. What d'you think?" she asked, meeting my eyes in the mirror.

I raked my gaze over her again. She stilled, then, very slowly, lifted her arms and raised her hair from her shoulders. The position outlined her body against the mirror, her breasts and ass thrust out. I waited until she released her hair, letting the black strands sift onto her shoulders, then took another sip of whiskey.

"That one," I told the saleswoman. "Wrap it up—and close the door on your way out."

The woman's thin dark brows arched knowingly. "Very good, sir."

She helped Lark out of the dress and draped it on a hanger. Then she gathered up the other dresses while I waited impatiently. At last the door closed behind her.

"Lock it," I told Lark.

She complied, her round ass swaying like a porn star's in the thong, and turned back to me.

I put my whiskey glass on the floor and came to my feet, spinning the chair to face the mirrors. "Bend over the chair."

She sauntered the few steps between us and fingered my lapel. "Yes, sir," she said in a dead-on imitation of the saleswoman's New York accent. "Whatever you say, sir." She fluttered her eyelashes at me.

I turned her around and lightly smacked her ass. "*Now,* Lark."

She bent over the chair, her palms on the seat. Without my asking, she widened her legs. "Like this?"

"Such a bad girl," I murmured as I slid my finger down the thong and between her cheeks. "You're soaked," I said, fingering her through the material. "You liked teasing me, didn't you?"

"Yeah." Her beautiful green eyes smoldered at me in the middle mirror. "I'm such a bad girl. I guess you'll have to spank me."

I cupped her mound. "If you want that salesperson hearing you begging me to stop..."

I should've known she'd see my dare and raise me one.

"How d'you know I wouldn't be begging you for more—harder?" she added on a whisper.

I gave her a firm tap right over her clit. "You are in so much trouble," I returned in an undertone. "But I'm not gonna spank you here. In fact, if you can't be quiet, I'll stop. Nobody gets to hear those sounds you make except me."

"I can be quiet." She started to pull down the thong but I stopped her.

"Leave it for now."

I rose back up so I could undo my belt buckle and dress pants. Lark was watching me in the mirror, so I gave her a show. Pushing down my pants and boxers but leaving them around my thighs. Fisting my dick and slowly stroking up and down. Running my thumb around the cap and lubricating myself with the pre-cum.

Her eyes darkened. Resting her weight on a forearm, she slid her free hand into her thong. Her salty, musky perfume filled my nostrils, and I heard the slickness as she moved her fingers in and out of her pussy.

I covered her with my body and cupped her tits. I toyed with her nipples, my gaze locked on the view of my hands in the mirror, tugging and playing the tight, rosy points.

"So damn sexy," I said next to her ear. "But can you be a good girl for me?"

A stifled moan escaped her closed lips, and I pinched a nipple. "What did I say about making noise?"

She squirmed, her bottom brushing over my erection. "I'm trying," she rasped.

"Try harder," I told her sternly, removing my hands from her breasts. "I give you an order, I expect it to be obeyed."

She drew a jagged inhale and dropped her voice to an almost-whisper. "Please don't stop. I'll be quiet—I promise."

"If you don't, you know what happens. Now let's get this

off." I removed her thong and touched my lips to the base of her spine.

She gave a little shiver. Something about me kissing that spot always set her off—and I loved that I knew that about her.

I gave a hard swallow. I was free falling off a tall building but fuck if I could save myself.

Even picturing Amina didn't hit me the same way these nights. Amina was in her final grave and had been for two decades.

Lark, though, was right here. I could touch her velvety skin. Bite her throat. Inhale her earthy female scent. Grip her waist and thrust into her so hard and deep it felt like we were connected in some profound, unexplainable way...

She pressed her bottom against my groin. "Make me come, Spider."

I wrapped my hand around her chin, forcing her head up. "No talking," I reminded her.

I actually didn't care if anyone heard us, but I got off on controlling her in this small way.

Her breath hitched and she nodded rapidly.

Taking myself in hand, I dragged the head through her wet folds. She made a maddening little circle, rubbing her clit over my hardness.

"That's it," I encouraged. "Get yourself off on me."

She squeezed her inner thighs around me and the pleasure was so intense, I had to bite back a growl. I rocked my hips, pushing between her thighs in slow, short strokes so she could use me how she wanted. But soon, it wasn't enough for either of us. She was panting and pushing against me, and I was so ready, I was going to come like a fifteen-year-old boy.

Pulling back, I dragged off the rest of my clothes and snagged a rubber from my wallet. I ripped the package open with my teeth, rolled it on with impatient hands, then lined up our bodies again.

She was too low, so I lifted her by the waist and put her on the carpet. "On your hands and knees."

She obeyed, her long black hair spilling over her shoulders. I knelt behind her and moved the silky mass aside, taking in her strong, sleek back, the indentation of her waist, the curve of her ass.

"So pretty," I said, low and gruff. I stroked her from her waist to her thighs, then back up her center, trailing my fingers from her pussy to the crack of her ass. I circled the tender pink pucker. "Someday, I'm gonna take you here."

She gave another of those sexy shivers. The next one, I wanted to feel with my whole body.

I covered her, filling my hands with her tits, and nudged inside of her. "Touch yourself. I want to feel you tighten around me while I'm fucking you." I waited until her hand was between her legs, then murmured, "Good girl."

Her pussy fluttered around me and I had to stifle my own groan.

"Look at you." I thrust slowly in and out of her. "You like that so much. My Lark would do anything to get fucked by me, wouldn't she?"

An eager nod.

"So sweet," I said, and gave a single hard stroke.

Her body tensed like a runner at the starting block.

"That's it," I muttered, picking up the pace. I would've kept going but Lark clenched on me, so ready, she was going to come soon.

And I wanted to see it on her face, to watch her come apart for me.

I stopped and pulled out, slapping her ass when she gave a muffled whine, then guided her to lie down on the thick pink carpet. She gazed up at me, heavy-eyed, knees bent, nipples rosy from me playing with them.

My beautiful, black-haired, smooth-skinned temptation.

I wanted to fall on her and take her like an animal.

I wanted to worship her like the gift from the gods she was.

Worship first, I decided, and slid down her body, searching for her swollen clit in with my mouth. I rubbed the flat of my tongue sideways and around it. Her hands came to my head, holding me where she wanted me. When her thighs tightened and started to quiver, I slid two fingers inside her and tickled that spot on the other side of her clit.

"Yesss," she hissed. "Spider…"

"Shh," I said, drawing her tender little nub into my mouth.

She bucked like I'd zapped her with an electric toy, constricting around my fingers as she came. I lifted my head in time to see her face stretched in ecstasy, eyes closed, mouth open in a silent scream.

I didn't give her time to regroup. Removing my fingers from her, I crawled on top of her, thrusting into her so hard her tits bounced. I sucked each tight, cherry-pink tip, then took her hands and stretched them above her head, holding them in place with one of my own. Her fingers curled around my hand, her thighs cradling my hips as I fucked her.

"Look at me," I ordered.

Her eyelids opened as if from a dream. Soft color tinted her cheeks, making her eyes appear even greener. A smile dawned on her face, crinkling her eyes and spreading to her mouth.

My fucking heart knotted. She looked so happy to see me. To be with me.

The shop door tinkled, and from the shop came the saleswoman's muffled voice. "Hello, Madam."

Lark moaned, and I released her hands and covered her mouth with my palm.

"Quiet," I warned.

She gave a cute growl—and bit my fingers.

I bared my fangs at her, saying, "Now you're in trouble." But I didn't mean it. I didn't want a kitten, I wanted a wildcat.

She struggled beneath me, trying to shake my hand off, but I just gave it to her harder until she stopped fighting, her hips raising to meet mine.

"That's it," I grated between my teeth. "Give me that hot pussy. Show me how much you want this."

She said something, her voice garbled, and I took my hand from her mouth, watching, fascinated, as a strip of blue glowed into life around her irises.

"More," she told me in a rough voice I barely recognized. "Give me everything."

Fuck, yeah. My last fragment of control snapped with an almost audible click. I lost myself, thrusting into her again and again.

A high, this-hurts-so-good cry burst from her lips. She babbled my name, interspersed with "yes," and "please."

Our gazes snagged. The world fell away. Even sound was muffled, like we were in a pink-and-black snow globe. I didn't hear the saleswoman or the customer or anything but the slap of our bodies and the low groans neither of us could help making.

I caught her wrists again, pinning them on either side of her head, my hips moving fast and hard now. She playfully bared her teeth at me, and I growled back.

"My woman likes to be held down," I said against her lips. "Doesn't she? She likes to know who she belongs to. Tell me. Tell me you're mine. That nobody's ever fucked you like this."

For a long moment she didn't speak. Then she said, "Yours," in that feral, sandpaper voice...and tightened around me in a second climax.

Pleasure detonated up my spine, my lungs emptying in a rush of air. I buried my face in the side of her neck and came with a drawn-out groan.

My lips opened, silently imprinting the word, "Mine," on her skin.

After, we cleaned up in the tiny bathroom attached to the dressing room. I finished first, then waited while Lark washed her face and finger-combed her hair.

I wrapped my arms around her waist. Her hair was messy, her cheeks still flushed, and she had a tiny mark on her throat where I must've scraped my teeth over her at some point.

The primal thing preened itself. "You look just fucked."

Our gazes locked in the mirror, and I braced myself for her to say something about that moment we'd shared. But she didn't, just gave me a Lark smirk. If I hadn't been looking straight at her, I wouldn't even have noticed that it didn't reach her eyes.

"That was hot. Like send-for-the-fire-engines hot."

"Mm," I said. I should've felt relieved that she was making it about sex. That was what I wanted, right? But instead of relief, I felt flat.

I moved her hair to the side, pressing a kiss to the delicate nob of her spine just above her shoulders. "Let's get outta here."

When we exited the dressing room, the saleswoman was waiting with the dress in a black garment bag, her expression carefully neutral. "If you need shoes, the shop next store has a good selection," she said as I handed her the cash for the dress.

"I do," said Lark, so we grabbed her a pair of high, pointy stilettos in the same purply red as the dress before heading back to the Cavern.

Velma caught up to us as I keyed in the code at the Chelsea Market entrance. She'd followed us at a discreet distance ever since we'd left the Underworld. I'd given up telling her not to; she never listened anyway. Anytime I was aboveground, she worried I was vulnerable.

Tonight, her thick dark hair was braided into a crown. In her fitted leather jacket, short black skirt and ankle boots, she looked like a hundred other women in lower Manhattan if you didn't know about the daggers strapped to her thighs beneath the skirt.

"Hey," she said to me with a nod in Lark's direction.

"Hey," I returned. "Everything alright?"

"Yeah. It's pretty quiet tonight. Want me to take that?" She reached for garment bag slung over my shoulder.

"Nah. I've got it."

The door swung open and we filed down the stairs, Velma in the lead and me bringing up the rear behind Lark. When we reached the Cavern, Lark held back after Velma went inside.

"Thanks for the dress and everything." She lifted the white-and-black bag holding her shoes.

I cupped her jaw with my free hand, tipping her face up for a kiss. "You're welcome."

As far as I was concerned, she'd already thanked me, but saying that was a little too much like she'd paid me in sex. Of course, she *was* paying me in sex. But not for the dress and shoes—that had been a gift.

And yeah, I'd made a mess of this.

That "Mine" I'd mouthed against her neck at the end? I'd meant it.

The rest of the Underworld would laugh their damn heads off if word got out that I'd blackmailed a woman into being my thrall—and then fallen for her.

Spider got caught in his own web.

Lark shifted from one boot-clad foot to the other. "I have something to ask you."

"What?" I stroked a thumb over her pillowy lower lip.

"I—you trust me now, right? You invited me to join your lair and all."

I pursed my mouth. It was a trick question because yeah, I trusted Lark. On the other hand, she was Grimclaw's cousin and I wasn't completely sure where her loyalties were.

Her face fell. "I see."

"Why d'you ask?" I hedged, releasing her.

"Because. It's been almost two weeks since you brought me back here."

"Yeah, so?"

"So am I still your prisoner? I mean, tonight was the first time since Halloween I've been outside the Cavern."

"Ah." I suppose I should've seen this coming, but I liked knowing that when I returned to the lair, she was waiting. That she was *safe*.

Maybe that was me being possessive, but that didn't mean she wasn't in danger. Something was clearly off, and until I knew what, the primal thing wouldn't be easy with her running around the Underworld.

Her mouth tightened. "Don't make me beg," she said as the silence drew out. "Not about this."

"I'm thinking," I muttered.

"I'm not going to run away. I mean, why would I? I need that twenty-five grand. I'm not going anywhere until you pay me. And you literally asked me to join your lair." She crossed her arms and jutted her chin, a mix of defiance and vulnerability. "Or would I still be your prisoner?"

My mouth turned down. I really didn't like being reminded that eventually, she'd leave, with me powerless to stop her, meaning she'd be out there, alone and unprotected.

But that wasn't what she was asking.

"No, you wouldn't be my prisoner."

She narrowed her eyes. "And now? I can come and go as I please?"

I expelled a breath. "Yes. I'll let Velma and the others know. But stick to this area. By now, the word's probably out that you're my...thrall. That makes you a target."

I'd almost said she was *my woman*. She didn't seem to catch it, though.

"Understood." She rose on her toes to kiss me. "Thanks, Spider-Dude."

Spider-Dude?

But I kinda liked that she had nicknames for me. Even Amina hadn't dared.

I wrapped my free arm around her waist and pulled her closer, making her arch her back, something she did with the ease of a dancer. "I'd say watch out for the booby traps," I said against her mouth, "but I don't think that's a problem for you."

Her bubbly, yeah-I'm-a-badass giggle coaxed a smile from me.

I dropped a kiss on her still-curved lips. "And be good, alright? Don't make me regret this."

"I won't. Scout's honor."

I snorted. "If you were a Girl Scout, then I'm a green-skinned elf."

Her smile increased. "Well, I *wanted* to be a Scout."

I shook my head at her and indicated the Cavern's door. "Lemme show you the combination."

14

LARK

Dressing-room sex might be my new favorite thing. Or should I say edgy, you-could-get-caught sex?

Not that the saleswoman would've let anyone walk in on us. She'd recognized Spider. I'd seen how she'd straightened when we entered the shop, Spider all smooth, hard-muscled power in a black leather jacket and blue silk shirt.

I'd also seen how the woman's eyes had eaten him up as she hustled over, beaming with welcome. She'd barely glanced at me in her eagerness to greet him.

Not that I blamed her. The man did look fine.

Anyway. My legs were still wobbly.

Even Spider threatening to stop if I couldn't keep quiet had been off-the-charts hot. There was something so sexy about him getting all alpha with me. And then in the end, he'd fucked me like he'd lost control...

Yeah, I'd done that to him.

Take that hungry-eyed saleslady.

I smothered a smile as I followed Spider through the Cavern. He opened the door to his bedroom and ushered me inside.

"Want this in the closet?" he asked, indicating the garment bag.

"I've got it." I took it from him and hung it in the walk-in closet. The shoebox I stowed on a shelf above.

Back in the bedroom, I found him closing his safe. I'd noticed he checked the contents at least once each night, making sure the dagger was safely in its box. Up until now, I hadn't said anything. Not my business, right?

But suddenly, I wanted it to be my business.

I came up behind him. "That dagger—it's special to you, isn't it?"

"Hm?" He turned around, his gaze inward.

"The dagger," I repeated. "It's special to you."

He focused on me. "Yeah."

I waited for him to add something, and when he didn't, wondered if I should back off. He clearly didn't want to talk about it.

But I felt something for him—and he felt something for me, I was sure of it. He'd called me "Mine," there at the end. He hadn't meant me to hear—he hadn't even said it out loud —but I'd felt his lips move and known that's what he was saying.

As for me, I'd been all-in on the "Mine" train.

"Give me everything."

I replayed that moment when I'd told Spider I was his, then begged him for more. For *everything*. Thank Luna, Spider believed it was only me caught up in the moment.

As for myself, I wasn't so sure what I'd been pleading for— or what primitive instinct had prompted me to say it.

But with the memory fresh in my mind, I asked the next question because I needed to know. "Was that Amina's?"

His eyes shuttered. "What d'you know about Amina?"

I swallowed, shrugged. "People talk."

He grunted, and I thought he wasn't going to answer me,

but after a pause, he said, "Amina gave me the dagger—had this lady bladesmith make it for me as a surprise."

My stomach dropped. The way his voice softened when he said her name...

And I'd stolen the dagger—a present from his lost love. No wonder he'd come after me himself.

Did he still love her? Had he meant to make her his mate like DeeDee seemed to think?

And if so, how was he still standing? For a supernatural, losing your mate was like having your heart carved out. Most of us followed our mates into their final graves within a month or two.

No, something inside me objected. *Not hers.*

Mine.

My eyes widened, my mind skittering away from the simple pronoun like it was a double-edged silver razor. Because if I was feeling possessive of Spider, what did that mean?

My expression must've given me away because he touched my cheek.

"I like you, Lark—a lot. More than anyone for a long time. But Amina got staked because of me." His Adam's apple bobbed, and my heart cracked a little for him. "Another alpha saw it as a way to strike me where I was weakest. When we buried her ashes, I swore I'd never put any woman in that kind of danger again."

I searched his rich brown eyes. "What're you saying?"

"That I'm not looking for a mate—or even a steady woman. It would be like painting a bull's eye on your—*her*—back."

"I...see."

But I didn't see, not really. That had been two decades ago. Spider had clearly grown as an alpha. He should be able to protect his woman, and it's not like I was completely helpless.

"I want you to stay," he said. "But I also wanna be upfront with you. Okay?"

"Yeah, sure. Appreciate the honesty." I dredged up a smile even though that crack in my heart was wide enough to fall into now.

I heard that he was trying to protect me, but I also heard that he was using me, just like Grimclaw had. Yeah, Spider wanted no-strings-attached sex, and Grimclaw had used me to enrich himself.

But being used is being used.

"Alright, then." He turned to leave.

I swallowed and decided the hell with smiling my way through this. "One question."

He halted, hand on the doorknob. "Yeah?"

"Do you think that's what Amina would've wanted? You spending the rest of your life alone?"

His fingers tightened on the knob so hard his knuckles went white. Then he blew out a breath. "I don't know. But it's what I want."

My stomach hollowed. I pressed both hands to it. "Right."

"Look, I'll see you later, okay?"

"Sure. I'm still your thrall until the month's up, right?"

That made his jaw tighten. Good—I'd meant it to hurt. Meant to jolt him, to remind him that this thing between us had an expiration date.

I held my breath, a part of me still hoping he'd...what? Tell me he was sorry, that Amina was his past.

But he just nodded and left, closing the door gently behind him.

Okay. I released a sad exhale, and reminded myself I couldn't stay anyway. Even if Spider begged me.

That didn't stop a couple of tears from sliding down my cheeks.

I scrubbed them away and headed into the shower. Because yeah, I felt like crap, but crying over some dude wasn't my style.

I WAS COMBING my hair when two quick knocks came on Spider's door. "Lark?" called Zayne. "Can we come in?"

"It's open," I called back, putting down the comb and returning to the bedroom.

Zayne entered along with DeeDee. I stiffened. DeeDee had dropped the overt aggression, but she was a human so I could sense her dislike. The feeling was mutual.

Zayne grinned at me. "How'd the shopping go?"

"Good." I let my mouth curve just to mess with DeeDee.

Zayne chuckled. "Now I know why Spider went with you."

DeeDee didn't smile, but for once, she wasn't giving off hate vibes.

"Show us what you bought," Zayne demanded.

"Yeah," said DeeDee. Her eagerness felt sincere, too.

"They're in the closet." They trooped after me into the walk-in closet, and I showed off the dress and shoes. After that scene with Spider, I wasn't as hyped about the Midnight Masquerade, but Zayne's squeal of delight and DeeDee's obvious envy helped.

Zayne took out the stilettos, examining the pointed toes. "They're La Scarpe's?" She eyed the box. "They as comfortable as people say?"

"Yep."

"They're perfect for your dress," chimed in Dee.

"Thanks." I zipped up the garment bag and hung it on a rail.

Zayne returned the shoes to their box and put them back on the shelf. "You buy a mask?"

"No. We...forgot." At that point, I'd still been in an orgasm-induced haze. I'd barely remembered to put on my underwear. "Where's a good place to buy one?"

"Abracadabra on Twenty-First Street," said Zayne.

"But I can make you one," DeeDee volunteered.

"Yeah?" I eyed her. "What would it look like?"

"She's good," Zayne confirmed. "And there's time, right? The Masquerade isn't until the end of the month."

DeeDee took out her phone. "Can I take a photo of your dress? I can match the style and color that way."

I wasn't sure I wanted DeeDee making my mask but I didn't see an easy way out, so I unzipped the garment bag again.

"How about something lacy?" She snapped a couple of photos.

I shook my head. "Too girly."

"I'm talking black-mesh lace. With wine-colored lace around the outside. Like this." She showed me a similar mask on her phone.

"That's...wow." The mask was gorgeous, dammit. And opaque enough to hide my features.

"I can make Spider a mesh mask, too. Not lacy—more edgy."

"All black," I said, giving in. "That would be great. I'll pay you, of course."

DeeDee gave me a razorblade of a smile. "Good, because I don't work for free."

Okay, there was the DeeDee I knew. I relaxed a bit. Nice DeeDee made me uneasy, but this version I could deal with.

"Then you have yourself a deal."

Back in the Cavern, I played a couple rounds of pool with Zayne, who was improving by the week, then put down my cue stick and slipped out the door.

I spent the first hour or so learning the area around Spider's lair—the tunnels, the cross passages, the spurs leading to nowhere. Of course, I had to avoid their trip wires and other traps, but that was kinda fun, like a real-life video game. The only cams were right outside the lair—I knew that from my previous recon. Why wire the tunnels with cams when you could set booby traps?

The whole time I was making my way to where I'd hidden my phone and the stolen jewelry. And yeah, I knew that checking your loot was a rooky mistake—best to forget about it until you were ready to retrieve it. But I wanted my phone.

So when I got close enough, I ducked into the shadows and zipped down a side corridor near Spider's lair. When I dropped back out of the shadows, I counted the tracks from a crack in the wall, stopping at the third track, where the phone was in a plastic bag covered by a layer of dirt. The jewelry in the bag under the fifth track, I ignored.

I was powering up my phone when Troll's mocking tones made me freeze.

"Well, look who's here, Grim."

I straightened from my crouch on the tracks and slipped the phone into my pocket, my gaze darting from him to my cousin.

The hair on my nape stirred. Grim looked like he hadn't fed for a week. His eyes bulged and his cheeks were hollow.

"Hey, Grim. What's up?"

Troll folded his beefy arms over his chest. He didn't look so good, either. "What's that in your pocket?" he countered.

"My phone."

"Show me."

I considered refusing, but it was two against one. "Fine. See?" I flashed it at Troll.

He snatched it from my hand and looked it over. "Why didn't you have it with you?"

"Well, hell, I don't know." I stuck out my hand for the phone and after a brief hesitation, he handed it over. I shoved it into my back pocket. "Maybe because I didn't want to chance losing it to Spider when I lifted his dagger. Who, by the way, chased me down and told me he owned me. Why would he think that, Grim?"

My cousin had the grace to look ashamed. Then his lip curled. "You landed on your feet, didn't you? Word is you're the kingpin's new pet, but he's still after me for his goddamn tribute."

"How is that my problem? You set me up, remember? As far as I'm concerned, you can go fuck yourself. Now, this has been real fun, but..." I started to fade into the shadows.

Troll grabbed my arm. If I didn't shake him off, I'd pull him into the shadows with me and he'd be able to track me. So I halted the fade.

"I'd stick around if I were you," he said, the corners of his lips curling into a predatory smirk. "We have info you're gonna want to hear."

My stomach plunged. "What?"

They moved in on me from either side, boxing me in against the tunnel wall. "Someone's offering a fuckton of money for you." Troll dug sausage-size fingers into my upper arm and gave me a shake. "You've been holding out on us, bitch."

Jared.

Nausea pressed into my throat. I licked my lips. "I don't know what you're talking about."

Grim snorted. "The name Darkman mean anything to you?"

"I know who they are, sure."

"Seems like Darkman, Junior has a jones for you."

Every instinct in me screamed, "*Run.*" But I could tell they were expecting that. That they wanted me to run.

Assholes.

I turned to my cousin. "Look, I get you need money. Maybe we can work something out."

15

SPIDER

My patience with Grimclaw had hit its limit.

The week I'd given him had been up yesterday, and he still hadn't paid the tribute. So after leaving Lark, I grabbed Velma and a couple of men and went to his lair, ready to drag the scumbag out by his scruffy neck and stake him. But he wasn't there, and the handful of vampires left in his lair swore they hadn't seen him or Troll for days. I ordered them out and blew up the entrance as a warning to anyone else who thought to jerk me around. His people, I told to either come up with the money I was owed or get out of Manhattan. They scurried off into the darkness like the rats they were.

Grimclaw and Troll were M.I.A. It figured that they'd bail, leaving their lair to face the music. Just in case, Velma alerted our crew to be on the lookout for them, and the two of us continued making the rounds of the lairs under my protection.

But Grimclaw apparently had a death wish, because as we left the fourth—and last—lair, Monster jogged up with a rumor that Grimclaw hadn't left my territory. "Looks like Troll's with him, too."

A fierce thrill shot through me. I flashed a cold smile. "Time to go hunting," I told Monster and Velma.

"I'll scout ahead in the shadows," Monster volunteered, his own teeth gleaming against his deep brown skin.

"Do it," I said, and started off with Velma following. For the first ten minutes, we didn't speak, aware of how voices carry in the Underworld's tunnels.

Velma broke the silence, speaking at a subvocal level only I could hear. "So you're taking Lark to the Midnight Masquerade."

The skin on my forehead pulled tight. I'd been expecting my friend to call me out on it. Hell, I was surprised she'd waited this long. That didn't mean I was ready to hear what she had to say.

"That's right," I replied in equally low tones. "So what?"

"So have you thought this through? You take a woman to something like that, she's not your thrall anymore."

"Says who? Half the vampires there are gonna be with a thrall."

"One they personally invited? One they took shopping for a dress and shoes?"

"It's just a dance. And she had nothin' to wear, alright? That's why I took her shopping."

And because Lark had sounded so sad when she'd explained why she didn't want to wear the gold dress.

"Riiiiiight." If you could hear an eyeroll, it would've sounded like Velma. "And how many other thralls have you taken clothes shopping? Or any other females, for that matter?"

We both knew the answer to that. I'd only taken one other woman shopping—Amina. Anyone else, I would've handed her a card and sent her out with one of my men.

I shot an irritated look at her over my shoulder. "Who made you my conscience?"

She shook her head. "Get a fucking clue, bro. You have feelings for her, don't you?"

"Fine," I muttered. "I do. Satisfied?"

"I like you, Lark—a lot. More than I have anyone for a long time."

But that made it even more crucial to pull back. To protect her from Amina's fate.

Velma sighed. "Lark's not Amina, you know. She's tougher. Amina was too sweet for her own good. The chick was the most human vampire I ever met."

My throat closed up. "Yeah," I said thickly.

"Hey. It's okay."

I slowed. "I knew it was a mistake," I said without looking at Velma. "That Amina wasn't going to last long in our world. Not at first, but by the end of that first year. That's why..."

"You didn't ask her to be your mate."

"Yeah." My chest heaved. "It felt...wrong."

And ever since, I'd had to live with the guilt, to wonder if I'd somehow led Amina on. Because I'd been the vampire who'd turned her.

I sped up again. "And Lark knows the deal, by the way. I told her I liked her but that I wasn't looking for a mate."

"Oh, Spider." She slipped past me and turned to face me, walking backward so I could see her pained expression. "You know that was an asshole thing to do, right?"

"I was being honest. You know, like women say they want."

She shook her head. "D'you *hear* yourself?"

I flashed on Lark's face, and the way her eyes had widened, her mouth turned down in a mix of sadness and shock.

My chest constricted. "Yeah."

Because now I'd said it aloud, I understood how it must've sounded to Lark. Arrogant. Clueless. Like this was only about sex when it had become more for both of us.

My 'honesty' had hurt Lark, too. She was good at hiding it, but that shine she'd had after we'd left the shop had dimmed.

I met Velma's eyes. "I fucked up, huh?"

"Depends."

"On what?"

"If she actually is your mate."

I halted and so did Velma.

"I like you, Lark—a lot."

Hell, *like* didn't come close to covering it. My need for Lark had grown teeth and claws. It tore at my insides, demanding me to stop pretending to myself that there was any planet where I'd let her walk away as promised.

I massaged my chest with my knuckles, trying to dig out the pain. But the sharp-toothed, clawed thing had already burrowed too deep.

"I can't—." I shook my head, swallowed. "I can't lose her like Amina."

"Hey. We both know there aren't any guarantees, bro." Velma moved closer and squeezed my shoulder, which was unusual in itself—Velma didn't like to be touched—her face soft with concern. "But you push her away, you're gonna lose her anyhow, and I think she's your true mate, the reason you never claimed Amina. There's something between you two— you just have to be in the same room and it's like sparks going off. We've all seen it. So get your head outta your ass and claim her before she takes off." She shook my shoulder and released me. "Okay?"

I tipped my head back, staring at the tunnel ceiling as if the answer might be written on the gritty concrete. "I dunno. I just don't fucking know."

Our phones buzzed in unison. Thankful for the interruption, I yanked mine out.

Velma stabbed a finger at me. "Think about, yeah?"

"I will, alright?" I grumbled, pulling up the message.

It was Jacko, informing us that Grimclaw and Troll had been seen about a half mile from the Cavern, at the outer edge of my lair's personal territory. He included a crossroads where we could meet him.

Velma's gaze locked onto mine over her phone, a quietly vicious satisfaction on her fine features. "Mr. Tiny Dick finally showed up."

Monster jogged up. "You heard?"

"About Grimclaw and Troll?" I said. "Yeah."

"Texting Jacko now," Velma muttered, fingers flying over her screen, "telling him we're on our way."

"Let's go." I broke into a run.

We sprinted the two miles to the crossroads in under five minutes. Jacko stepped out of the shadows, halting us. "There." He jabbed a finger around the corner.

Velma and I peered down the tunnel. Lark was huddled with Grimclaw and Troll, speaking in hushed tones.

Velma stiffened. "What in the name of the Kali?" she said under her breath.

Lark's voice rose. "I can get the money, okay? Just give me a few days to work on him."

She might as well have lobbed a live grenade at me. My initial shock morphed into fury. I slid my dagger from the holster on my belt loop and stalked toward them, Velma behind me and Jacko flitting ahead and to the side.

Behind us, Monster whispered, "I'll be in the shadows."

I barely registered what he'd said over the angry buzzing in my head, but I managed a tight nod.

Lark spun around, hand flying to her mouth. Her guilty expression added gasoline to the fire in my chest.

"Spider. I—"

The buzzing increased to the roar of a thousand drones. I grabbed her and pushed her at Velma. "Shut up and wait with Velma."

"It's not what you th—"

My growl came from the primal, feral place. "I told you to shut the fuck up."

Grimclaw and Troll stared at us, open-mouthed but somehow satisfied, too.

"And you?" I told them. "You're dead. You should've gotten outta here when the rest of your lair did."

Grimclaw whitened. "I didn't mean anything. I just wanted to see my cousin before I left."

Meanwhile Troll sidled sideways, putting space between himself and his alpha, the coward. I ignored him, trusting Velma and Monster to secure him, and drove Grimclaw into a niche in the subway wall. Jacko backed me up.

"Wrong answer," I told him. "I warned you to stay away from her, didn't I?"

Lark made a small sound. "You did what?"

I whipped my head around. "Not another word, understand? Velma—gag her if you have to."

Lark lifted her palms, easing backward. "Fine. I'll be quiet, alright?"

Velma clamped a hand on her arm, and Monster had gotten a hold of Troll.

But when I turned back to Grimclaw, Monster cursed and I glanced around to see that Troll had taken off, Monster on his heels.

"Troll, dammit!" Grimclaw tried to follow Troll.

I poked his chest with my blade. "Stay."

He froze. "Please, my lord. I just wanted to see my cousin. What's so wrong about that?"

"It's wrong because I say it is. I told you she was dead to you. What part of that meant you get to visit her whenever the fuck you feel like it?"

Velma frowned at her phone. "Troll went into the shadows. Monster says be careful."

I jerked my head in acknowledgment. Nearby, I sensed Lark coming a step closer. A part of me would always know exactly where she was. "Spider, please. Just listen to me."

Her pleading tones made me feel like the biggest fool in the world because I wanted to give in. Wanted to trust her. Wanted to believe she hadn't been playing me all this time.

I snapped my head around. "Dammit, Velma. Keep her quiet."

Velma folded her arms over her chest. "I think you should hear what she has to say."

Lark's pretty throat worked. The same throat I'd kissed just a few hours ago. "It's not what you think," she said before I could say anything else. "I'm on your side."

"Are you? Because it didn't sound like that to me. Sounds like you were all about getting what you could from me. How much were you gonna ask for this time? Fifty grand? A hundred? Because baby, you're not *that* good."

"Stop it!" A furious blue lit up around Lark's green irises. She glared at me, hands clenched, a streak of red on each of her cheekbones. "We were just talking, you jerk. He's my cousin, for Luna's sake."

"That's what I told him," Grimclaw muttered.

I silenced him with a look. To Lark, I said, "I heard you, you little hustler. You told him you could get the money, that you just needed a few days to work on me."

She took a long breath. "Okay, I admit that looks bad. But I didn't mean—"

Lark gasped as Troll emerged out of the shadows behind Velma, a silver blade raised high. He slashed it down toward her nape, aiming for that spot beneath her skull that would severe her spine.

My heart lurched. Even a vampire can't recover from a blow like that.

"Velma!" I shot forward. "Behind y—!"

But I was too far away, and to get to Troll, I'd have to go through Velma first. The silver arced through the air and I realized sickly that I wasn't going to be able to reach Troll in time. My only hope was to knock Velma to the tracks.

Lark was right beside Velma, though, and she moved at the same time, screaming Troll's name as she gave him a hard shove, knocking him off-balance. He stumbled, his knife slicing into Velma's right shoulder instead of her spine.

A split second later, I slammed into Velma, taking her down to the berm beside the subway tracks. I rolled with her, taking the brunt of the impact, then leapt to my feet to find Lark facing down Troll with the switchblade I'd allowed her to keep. It was only a matter of time before he got through her defenses.

My stomach dropped to my boots. I was dimly aware of Jacko pinning Grimclaw to the wall, but I was already in motion.

I didn't care that Lark might be an empty box of lies tied up with a pretty, witchy-eyed, black-haired ribbon. The primal thing knew she had to be protected.

I hurtled across the tracks, grabbing her by the waist and carrying her past Troll. His blade flashed in the dim light. The motherfucker had nearly skewered her.

I set Lark on her feet and turned to Troll. "You're going down," I said in hoarse tones I barely recognized as mine.

"No." Velma's voice. "The sucker's mine."

She'd gotten back on her feet. Her right arm was useless, but she'd taught herself to fight with either hand. She stalked toward Troll, murder in her eyes.

For a big man, he moved fast. He dodged left, and Velma missed his chest but slashed open his bicep to the bone. His blade clattered to the subway track. He swept it up with his good hand and took off running, leaving his alpha to face us on his own.

Like I said, the man was a coward.

Velma took a few steps after him, then turned back, a hand clamped to her bleeding shoulder. She slumped against the wall, chest working. "Can't," she muttered through pale lips.

Monster raced up, his gaze taking in Velma's injury and a white-faced Lark. "What the fuck?"

"Get Troll," I barked, pointing down the track.

"Text Zayne," I ordered Velma. "Tell her we need help. And you." I pointed a finger at Lark. "Don't even think about moving."

Her breasts heaved. "Whatever."

Jacko had Grimclaw cornered, but as soon as he released him, the man tried to fade. Jacko swore and grabbed his arm, anchoring him in the physical world.

"Enough." Shooting forward, I wrapped my fingers around his face and slammed his skull back against the tile behind him. The thud echoed dully in the tunnel.

"Help Velma," I told Jacko. "I can handle this mofo."

Zayne skidded around the corner, blades out.

"Secure Lark in the Cavern," I ordered her without releasing Grimclaw.

Zayne frowned at my rigid, tight-lipped thrall. "What d'you mean, secure Lark?"

"I mean throw her into a goddamn cell. Something's funny, and until I know she's not some kinda plant, I want her under lock and key."

Zayne seemed frozen in place. She glanced from Lark to Grimclaw to me.

"Oh-kay," the red-haired dhampir said.

"No!" Lark's eyes begged me to listen. "I'm not a plant! You've got this all wrong."

"Zayne." My head was buzzing again. My back teeth clenched. "Get her out of here. *Now.*"

Zayne swallowed audibly. Then she grabbed Lark's arm. "You heard the alpha. Move."

Lark sent me a last look over her shoulder, eyes shimmering with tears. Then her mouth hardened. She dragged the back of her hand across her eyes and left.

The buzzing in my head increased, and I knew who was going to pay for it. I released Grimclaw's face to pull out my dagger.

His eyes bugged in fear. "Hey, take it easy."

My smile was more of a grimace. I dug it into his throat, taking satisfaction in the blood that welled up along. The burning odor of the silver scorching his skin just made me happier. "You should've got outta New York while you had a chance."

"You got it all wrong, my lord. Lark sent for me."

"That's a lie!" Lark called out from down the tracks. "They were waiting for me."

Zayne pulled her around the corner.

Grimclaw licked his lips. Even aside from his burnt-skin odor, the man smelled rank, and he looked worse. "Look, you can have in on this if you want. Lark's got a line on a buttload of cash."

I poked him with the blade. "Explain."

Greed sharpened his face. "What's it worth to you?"

"Bloody Hades," I said in disgust. The man was the worst sort of rat. "She's your goddamn cousin."

His eyelids flickered. "Or we can split the cash. No problemo. I owe you anyhow."

My fingers tightened on the dagger's handle. I wanted to end Grimclaw so bad I could taste it. "What cash?"

He considered me, then his face closed up. "I need some assurances first."

"You don't get to ask for assurances, punk." I unbuttoned the coat of his beige leisure suit and tore a hole in his ratty white shirt with my dagger, baring his chest to me. "The three of you were having a convo and I wanna know what about."

He worked his jaw from side to side. "Benjamins," he spat at me. "That's what she always wants. I bet she took you for a few grand, right?"

More like twenty-five grand.

"Thought so," he said with a knowing, man-to-man smile that made me want to slice his lips off his face. "Well, you must not have coughed up enough because she wanted to know what we'd pay for the code to your lair."

I stilled. Lark wouldn't.

But how did Grimclaw know she had the code? Unless he'd been in the shadows watching when I'd shown it to her…

"Huh." He eyed me pityingly. "You think she should be loyal to you 'cause you stuck your magic dick in her? She's out for herself, dude. Always has been. Always will be. For enough money, she'll do anything, including let us pick you all off while you're still half awake."

What if he was telling the truth?

He's not. Lark wouldn't do that.

"Like fuck she would." That was Velma from her seat on the ground where Jacko was examining her wound.

Grimclaw shot her a glance and flinched. He tried to hide it, but I saw and so did Velma, judging by her rusty chuckle.

"Lark's no angel," my friend added. "We dug up enough on her to know that. But doing us like that isn't her style—she's not the violent sort. Besides, she's happy with us. Anybody can see that."

"That's what she wants you to think," Grimclaw retorted.

I dug my dagger into his solar plexus. The silver seared another hole in his skin, and he whined in pain. I left it there another few seconds, then eased off on the pressure without removing it completely.

"I'm not interested in your opinion of your cousin," I told him. "Although if that's what you think of her, no wonder she wants out of your lair."

His face set. "Yeah? Well, stop poking me with that blade or I'm not tellin' you nothing. And I want a guarantee I walk free."

"A guarantee? Sure, you got it." I said without saying *what* I'd guaranteed, which was nada. "Now talk."

"The dagger," he reminded me tightly, and I pulled it back an inch, keeping it pointed at his chest.

"So which is it?" I prompted. "The woman needs cash so bad she's gonna sell out my entire lair? Or she's got a buttload of cash?"

His eyelids flickered. Yeah, the punk was definitely playing me.

"She has money," he said, his lower lip sticking out like toddler's. "Somewhere. I know she does. Her parents were loaded. So where is it now? I figure you can make her tell us."

"Do you?" I said softly.

He gulped, but didn't back down. "Yeah. The bitch told me it had all been lost in some big bet that they didn't pull off."

He seemed outraged that Lark might've held out on him, even though it was clear he would've relieved her of any money in the blink of an eye if he could've.

I considered him, contemplating whether squeezing any more info out of him was worth the effort. The man wouldn't know the truth if it morphed into a Rottweiler and bit him on his bony ass. He was playing me, flipping his tale every time it left his mouth.

That didn't mean there wasn't a kernel of reality buried somewhere in there. But I could get that from Lark or Troll.

He shifted uneasily. "Are we done here?"

"Yeah," I said and punched the blade into him, angling it upward so it went deep into his heart. "That's for jerking me around." I gave the dagger a twist. "And that's for treating Lark like a fucking slave."

His mouth opened in shock. He grasped the handle, tugging weakly, but he couldn't dislodge it. "You stupid bastard," he grated, blood bubbling from the corner of his lips. "She's worth money, I tell ya."

"I don't need her money."

"Yeah? Well, you don't know who you're dealin' wi—" His eyes rolled up in his head and his breath rattled out. He groaned and, mercifully, went silent.

"Yeah?" I jerked the blade from his chest and wiped it on his leisure suit. "From where I'm standing, you forgot who *you're* dealing with. Because you seem to think I'm a weak-ass alpha—like you."

I stepped back, watching as he staggered sideways, then stumbled into the wall and slid to the tunnel floor, his body smoking. A few seconds later, his chest burst into dark flames, consuming him from the inside out. The tunnel filled with the rank smell of charred flesh.

I turned to Jacko, who'd been doing his best to keep Velma from jumping to her feet to help me. "Velma okay to move?"

She answered me herself. "Please," she said with a look of disgust at Grimclaw's disintegrating body. "Get me outta here."

Together, we helped my injured lieutenant to her feet and to the Cavern door. Inside, I took over, guiding her to a couch with an arm around her waist.

"I'll clean her wound," Jacko volunteered, striding to the kitchen for supplies.

"You sure you're alright?" I asked Velma. "Because I need to talk to Lark."

She rolled her eyes. "It's just a scratch. But come here." She beckoned me closer, and when I bent down, she hissed, "Chill, big man. Before you do anything, ask Lark why she met up with those two asses."

My mouth turned down. "I know why. She's his cousin. I'm the dude who's paying her to have sex with me. Guess who's side she's on?"

"She *likes* it here, you idiot. There's something we don't know."

"Maybe," I said.

The conditions Lark had been living in flashed into my mind, piercing the rage and disappointment that had been driving me ever since finding her with her cousin and his lieutenant. Why would any sane person pick Grimclaw over me? Added to that cryptic comment Grimclaw had made about Lark being worth money and Velma was right.

Something was very off. I'd known all along Lark was keeping secrets. I'd even suspected she was on the run from whoever had staked her parents.

Well, she wasn't getting out of that cell until she told me everything. Like it or not, she was under my protection now, and if her secrets had landed her sexy ass in danger, that was unacceptable on every fucking level.

I crouched next to Velma, running a practiced eye over her injured arm. It had stopped bleeding, but the silver blade had left a nasty gash. "You sure you're okay?"

She leaned back against a cushion. "What, am I some fragile flower? Go to her already."

I picked up her hand. "If you promise you won't get up the second my back's turned."

She wrinkled her nose at me, but I could tell she was touched that I cared. "Fine. I promise, alright?"

"Good." I squeezed her fingers and strode off.

By then, word must've gotten out about the attack because most of the lair had gathered in the Cavern's great room. But as I made my way through the small crowd, not a single person tried to stop me.

16

LARK

Zayne herded me through a labyrinth of poorly lit passages that I'd never been in. "What in Hades did you do?"

"Nothing," I bit out. "All I did was talk to my cousin and his lieutenant. I didn't even know they were gonna be out there—they were waiting for me."

"Then why is Spider so pissed off?"

"He heard me tell my cousin and his lieutenant that I could get money from him. I was just trying to get them off my back, but Spider showed up at exactly the wrong time."

"Oh. And he doesn't believe you?"

"I don't know. He wouldn't let me explain." Anger and frustration welled up inside me, turning my stomach into a tight knot.

We passed DeeDee's bedroom. She was smiling down at an iPad, but she glanced up as we passed and met my eyes. Her smile faded, but I could sense her predominant emotion, and inside, she was happy-dancing that I was in trouble.

Bitch.

DeeDee put down the device and scrambled to her feet. "Need any help?" she asked Zayne, who shook her head.

"I've got it."

DeeDee followed us into the hall and stayed there, watching until we turned down a short hall with only one room, its thick door ajar.

Zayne nudged me inside. "Look," she said, "I'll keep an ear to the ground, see if I can find anything else. But if I were you, when Spider shows up, I'd grovel. Tell him you're sorry, that you didn't mean it."

I threw up my hands. "But I *didn't* mean it. It was a lie."

"Then you just have to tell him that, okay?"

"Yeah, sure. I'll tell him. Again." I took in the sagging cot, pink Formica table and a pair of chrome chairs with cracked yellow vinyl seats, and my shoulders sagged. "Just...don't let them forget I'm in here, okay?"

"I won't." Zayne hesitated, then squeezed my shoulder. "It will be okay, you'll see." She closed the heavy, silver-reinforced door behind her.

"Sure," I said as the room went dark. On the other side of the door, a bolt slammed into place.

I made my way to the table where I'd glimpsed a squat candle just before the door shut. I felt around the base, relieved to find it was battery-operated. I flipped the switch, and it lit up, a spot of gold in the grimy cell.

Skirting the table, I opened the room's only other door to find a toilet and a ceramic sink that appeared to have been rescued from a dumpster.

"Well," I muttered to myself. "Beggars can't be choosers."

I sank onto the cot. The metal frame creaked in protest.

A bitter taste filled my mouth.

So much for Spider asking me to join his lair.

Hell, so much for trust. Spider had immediately believed the worst of me, and probably Velma and Monster, too. Even

Zayne had seemed doubtful, although at least she'd been willing to listen to my side.

Dad always said the only people we could rely on were ourselves. We three against the world.

But my parents had used me, too. As soon as I hit my mid-teens, I'd been their shill, the barely legal bait dangled in front of vampires to score invites to exclusive syndicate parties.

Then they'd decided to go big and "sold" me to the Darkman Syndicate.

Yeah, my own parents had inked a deal with Jared Darkman—a million dollars in return for a month with me.

"Easiest cash I ever made," my dad had said in satisfaction as he showed me the briefcase full of bills.

I'd gaped at them. "Are you out of your minds?! How could you do this without asking me?"

Mom paused in the act of touching up her scarlet lipstick. Blond and ethereally beautiful, she wrinkled her nose at me in the mirror.

"But he's never going to have you," she said, like that made it okay. "We'll take the money and move to Europe. We can live as humans until things cool down."

I'd backed away, furious and frightened. "You're wrong. Jared's not going to give this up. He wants me, and he's used to getting whatever he wants. I've barely been able to hold him off."

"We can handle him," my father said with his typical confidence. The son of a Spanish baron and his mistress from back when being a Spanish nobleman meant something, there was little he didn't believe he could handle.

I turned on him. "I *trusted* you. I trusted both of you. I thought we were a team. You have to clear these things with me first. I'm not a-a toy you can wave at a man, then snatch away."

"Calm down," said my father.

Calm down? A red haze filled my vision.

"I'm not gonna do it," I'd said and stomped into my connecting room. Behind me, I could hear Dad telling Mom to give me a little time, I'd come around.

Fuck that.

I'd shoved a few things into a plastic bag and jumped off my balcony. I'd been on my way out of Vegas when Jared and a half-dozen enforcers had stormed into our hotel suite.

My mom had managed to get off a message to me. "Stay low," she'd said. "We'll contact you."

And that was the last thing I'd heard from either of them. I'd wasted a couple of precious nights, dithering about going back, but they would've contacted me if they were still alive. And then every bit of money had been transferred out of all five of our joint accounts and I'd known Jared hadn't just gotten to them, he was after me, too.

I pressed both hands to my belly, still sick at how it had all fallen out.

Turns out, Jared was the kind of dude who held a grudge. He wasn't going to let this go until he'd had that month from me, and now, he'd apparently put a bounty out on me.

I scrubbed my hands over my face, exhausted clear to my bones. I was so tired of just trying to survive.

Maybe it was time to stop running. I'd lost my parents over this, although that had been due to their damn greed. I didn't want to lose Spider, too. Already, Velma had been injured because of me.

At least with Jared, I wouldn't have to worry about falling in love. Because, yeah I was in love with Spider.

And you know what? Being in love sucked.

A thorny ache prickled my throat. I sat back, eyes stinging, chest tight.

Hating Grim and Troll. Hating Jared even more. But most of all, hating that this was the end for me and Spider.

He was the best thing that had happened to me in...well, ever. I refused to take him and his lair down with me.

Because I had to get out of here...and let Jared find me.

A tear slid down my cheek. I dug my fingernails into my thighs, squeezed my eyes shut.

Chill, Lark. It's just another scam, right? Well, maybe not a scam, but you'll be playing a part—the vampire prince's pretty, brainless thrall.

My stomach made a high dive off a board into an empty pool.

Jared Darkman had a worse reputation than Spider. He also had a whole fucking syndicate behind him. We'd poked the bear. Well, my parents had, anyway, and he wanted his revenge. He was going to do his level best to break me.

"Aw, ain't you sweet?"

My eyes flew open. Troll leaned against the rough stone wall next to the door, a hand clamped over his bloody bicep. He was pale beneath his natural tan, but he managed a sneer.

"Tell me, are you crying over Spider—or what Darkman's gonna do to you?"

My heart simply...stopped. Then it came back online, beating triple time.

I came to my feet. "How did you get in here?"

"I was right with you the whole time. Spider's gotten complacent. Thinks no one's got the guts to break into his precious Cavern. Which means it's just you and me, sweet cheeks."

Just in case I didn't understand, he slid his uninjured hand down to his groin and cupped it.

An involuntary shiver shook me.

His mouth curled in a sly grin. "Nothin' to say?"

"Just that you must have a death wish, because when Spider finds you in here, you're toast."

"He won't. No one saw me come in here."

"Or he's letting you think that," I retorted.

A hint of uncertainty darkened Troll's square face. He darted a look around the cramped cell.

I pressed my point. "Spider's smart. If I were you, I'd get out while you can. There are cams everywhere," I added, even though I hadn't seen any inside the Cavern.

Troll shrugged. "If he knew I was in here, he'd have already come. And neither of us is leaving until they open that." He nodded at the locked door.

I shook my head like I knew better, but he was right, of course. I'd just been trying to crack his confidence. Make him nervous and he might back off.

"No, we're alone." Troll looked me over like he was mentally tearing off my clothes. "And I wanna taste of that high-class pussy of yours. See what the fuss is about."

"Yeah?" I slid my switchblade from my sock. "Come any closer and this high-class pussy will cut off your fucking dick and shove it into your mouth."

Troll winced, then took a menacing step forward to make up for it. "Does Spider know about Darkman?" His eyes narrowed. "No, of course not. He has no clue, does he? You didn't even tell us."

"So? There's a lot of things I haven't told you."

"Two million big ones. That's what Darkman's payin'."

My jaw unhinged. "Two million?"

"You heard me." Troll pushed off the wall and prowled toward me. "Although I betcha I could get him to up the ante. He's hell-bent on dragging you back to Vegas. Something about punishing you for leading him on."

I circled sideways, aware he was trying to box me in.

He circled with me, his injured arm hugged to his side. It had stopped bleeding, but a silver injury like that would take days to heal. Troll didn't seem worried, though. He seemed to think he could take me one-armed.

Unfortunately, he was probably right. The man was damn strong if he'd managed to stay in the shadows that long despite the silver poisoning his blood.

I darted a glance at the cell door. Where the fuck was Spider?

Troll crowded me into a corner between the cot and the wall.

I tightened my grip on the switchblade handle. "Back off, or I *will* cut you."

He tsked. "You'd cut your own lieutenant?"

I stiffened. "You're not my lieutenant anymore."

"I am if I say I am, little girl. But make it good for me, and maybe I'll tell Darkman I couldn't find you." His breath had gotten heavier, his eyes encircled with neon blue.

My back teeth clamped together at that 'little girl.' "Fuck you," I said and shot past him, intentionally jostling his hurt arm.

"*Bitch.*" He stalked after me.

I danced around the table, trying to keep it between us. "You must think I'm an idiot. Whatever I do, you'll sell me to Darkman. At least this way, I don't have let you stick your dick in me."

He snarled and lurched sideways, forcing me into another corner.

I tried to slip past him, but he had me blocked in now. My heart sank.

It was clear I was on my own, that no one was going to rescue me. What had I expected? Spider could've decided to leave me down here for a couple of days to stew.

And I couldn't evade Troll much longer. It was either fight or be raped.

And to be real, I wasn't much of a fighter. I could hold my own, but my family was all about the hustle. You got in a bad spot, you talked your way out. You didn't fight your way out.

Troll leaned in. "Darkman knows about Spider. He has someone on the inside feeding him intel about you. He's been waiting for you to leave the Cavern, but Spider's kept you locked down. So he contacted Grimclaw, worked out a deal."

My mouth dried. "No. You're lying! Spider's crew wouldn't sell him out like that."

"He offered one million to start. Grimclaw made him raise it."

He offered the information like that made Grim some kind of saint or something. For enough money, Grimclaw would sell his own mother out.

I sneered. "Guess he was kicking himself for only taking Spider for that twenty-five thou he owed as tribute—"

Troll's hand shot out, plucking the dagger from my hand. In the next instant, he had me pinned to the wall as he threw my blade to the floor. "You'll do everything I ask, and you'll do it with a fucking smile." He rocked his hips against my stomach, making sure I felt his erection. "Because if you don't, I'll let Darkman and his enforcers into the Cavern."

I swallowed sickly. I'd done this. I'd brought Darkman down on Spider and his people.

I lifted my chin. "Go ahead. See if I care."

"You wanna test me? If you don't care about these people, then why were you sitting there looking like you'd lost your last friend? And why'd you save Velma out there? I owe you for that, by the way."

He reared back like a cobra, his upper body curved, and backhanded me across the face.

Stars exploded behind my eyes. I swallowed a moan and brought my hand to my cheek. For a few seconds, I couldn't breathe, and it felt like he'd split my lip open. I dragged in a breath and worked my jaw back in forth, sucking the blood from my lip. Troll's eyes sparkled with an unholy blue light, his vampire getting off on seeing me bleed.

"Darkman's gonna get his new toy one way or the other," he told me. "But it's your choice. Are you gonna cooperate with me or d'you want to see him kill all your new friends first?"

My heart folded in on itself. Troll was a dickhead, but he was right. I had a choice here.

I'd done this. It was up to me to make it right.

"Chill, would you?" I said as calmly as I could. "I mean, d'you really think I'd choose them over me? Spider's paying me to fuck him. I made my own bargain with him."

Troll's eyelids flickered.

"What? You think I'd still be here if I wasn't getting something out of it?"

He needed to see me as a complete mercenary, out only for herself. Someone who'd sell her soul if the price was right. If I couldn't save myself, at least I'd save Spider and his lair.

"Work with me," I urged. The words felt oddly shaped in my mouth, like they were being spoken by someone else. "We can both win here. The Darkmans are billionaires. Two million is nothing to them."

Troll considered me, and I had a flash of hope. Maybe I was getting through to him?

"I'll take it under consideration." He pushed me toward the cot. "But first, get on that bed and prove how much you want to work with me."

My stomach knotted. I lowered myself to the mattress's edge, mind blank.

Troll pulled out his own switchblade. "Pants off, little girl."

I fumbled with the top button of my jeans.

Survive. Focus on that. Survive so that someday, you can stake this sonuvabitch.

I reached for my zipper...and stilled as the door rattled, followed by the unmistakable sound of the bolt sliding.

Troll muttered a curse. He grabbed my shirt and said, "Say anything and whoever walks in that door is a dead fuck."

Then, with a visible effort, he faded back into the shadows, faster than should've been possible with his injury. Before he disappeared, he pointed his index and middle fingers at first his eyes, then at me.

I'm watching you.

~

THE DOOR SEEMED to take an hour to swing open. I scrambled to my feet, hurriedly rebuttoning my jeans.

Spider filled the doorway. Relief whooshed through me, even when he halted, hands gripping the door frame, his eyes hooded, face carved out of hard, unforgiving stone.

He was angry. But I knew him well enough now to know he was disappointed, too. His mouth was turned down like he'd swallowed something sour.

But he'd come. He'd saved me, even if he didn't know it. I gave him a smile that trembled at the edges, aware of Troll watching us from somewhere in the cell.

Spider finally spoke. "Can I trust you, Lark? That's what I want to know."

I recoiled, blinking rapidly. Inside, I died a little. That he felt he had to ask.

Yeah, I was a hustler and a thief—I was used to being blamed when things went south. But damn it, this time, I'd been *trying*.

I *liked* these people. I'd never do anything to hurt them, and it was like a fist to the gut to have to defend myself.

Anger surged up in me, heating my face. For a few seconds, I forgot about Troll listening. "Fuck you."

"That's not an answer."

I clenched my fists. "I saved Velma. That should be answer enough for you."

Spider's brow lowered. "Doesn't mean I can trust you. You could be lying your ass off and still save someone."

"Fine, you can't trust me. I mean why should you? I'm just some thrall you're paying for sex."

He absorbed that, tight mouthed. "So it was all about the money?"

Wow. Talk about a body blow. That thing inside me that felt like it was dying curled in on itself defensively.

You know it was more. Nobody's that good at faking it.

Belatedly, I recalled Troll was listening. I drew a deep breath and reminded myself that it didn't matter what Spider thought of me. That what was at stake was bigger than either of us.

Troll had meant it when he'd said he'd let Darkman and his enforcers into the Cavern. For all I knew, they were somewhere nearby right now. I had to play this Troll's way until I knew more.

So I met Spider's eyes—and lied. The way I'd been taught. Not overselling it, just explaining.

"We had some fun, okay? But that's all it was. You told me yourself it couldn't be anything else."

"And Grimclaw? Why'd you tell him you'd get money from me?"

"To get him off my back." I slit my eyes at him. "What d'you care? It's my money, right? What I do with it at the end of the thirty days is none of your damn business."

Spider's gaze turned inward. "So he threatened you with something." His lids lifted as he worked it out. "What?"

I managed a nonchalant shrug. "Grim's always threatening something. That's why I'm outta here as soon as I work out my contract with you."

He let out such a nasty growl that I jumped a little. "He told me you have a line on a lot of cash. What did he mean by that?"

I spread my hands. "How should I know? Ask him."

"I did. But he kept changing his story. So now I'm asking you."

I shook my head, fresh out of lies.

"Lark. I wanna help. At least tell me what's going on—you owe me that much, don't you?"

I moistened my lips. Luna help me, I wanted to agree.

But this wasn't about me. This was about saving Spider from Jared, and even Troll, because any minute, Troll was going to be forced to drop out of the shadows, and then he'd attack.

I had to get Spider to leave, and suddenly, I knew exactly how to do it. He'd handed me the reason himself.

"Dude," I said, sauntering toward him. "Get over yourself. I don't owe you anything I'm your thrall, remember? Your prisoner."

He went rigid, his brown eyes glittering with fury and hurt.

The hurt nearly did me in, but I drew a breath and plowed on. "I've been your good girl in bed, haven't I? Did everything you asked. So why the third degree? If I wanna talk to my cousin, it's none of your freaking business."

His fingers gripped the doorjamb so tight the thick wood groaned. "I trusted you."

"Did you?" I was close enough to touch him now, and the urge to do so was so strong, I crossed my arms over my chest to stop myself from following through. Not an angry pose, a protective pose, with my hands fisted and tucked under my upper arms. "You wouldn't even let me leave the Cavern until I begged you. You have people watching me all the time. If that's trust, I'd like to see what not trusting me looks like."

A muscle jumped in Spider's cheek. "That's called protection, dammit. You admitted yourself you're hiding from someone."

He'd been protecting me?

For a heartbeat, I just stared at him. Then I shook my head.

Not that I didn't believe him. But I was still caught up in selling the lie because he couldn't get involved in this.

Spider grabbed my upper arms. I thought he was going to shake me, then his nostrils flared. "Who hit you?"

My mouth opened and shut.

"Tell me, dammit. Unless—" He tensed. "Was it one of my people? Because—"

"No!" Too late, I realized I should've lied. I couldn't accuse Troll, after all. But I couldn't bring myself to finger an innocent person. "It was during the fight," I hurried to say. "I fell, remember?"

He bit out a curse. "The truth, Lark."

I pressed my mouth together, shaking my head.

He growled. Then to my shock, he enfolded me in a hug, my unhurt cheek against his chest. "Okay, forget that for now. Who's after you, baby? Let me help you." His voice softened. "You can trust me. I'm on your side."

I dragged in a deep breath. I never wanted to forget how Spider smelled.

Then I pushed at his chest. "I told you, this is business. So if you want to fuck, at least get me out of here so we can do it on a clean mattress."

"Business?" He recoiled and released me. For an endless moment, we just stared at each other.

This was it. The end.

Inside, my heart pounded and thrashed like it wanted to leap out of my chest and beg him not to believe me, that it was one big lie. I pressed the heel of my hand against my breastbone, willing my headstrong heart—and my mouth—to stay silent.

He broke the stand-off first. "You don't mean that," he said with a pointed look at the hand I had against my chest.

I let my arm fall back to my side, my voice hardening. "Yeah. I do."

17

SPIDER

I almost left. I almost believed Lark's crap.

I mean, it fit.

The background check we'd run had been enough to prove she had a checkered history. With the aid of a facial recognition app, Monster had found multiple aliases: Lark as a fancy thrall in a tight red dress, her hair dyed blond and piled on top of her head. Lark as the down-to-earth girl-next-door in a T-shirt and jeans, hair in a long red braid. Lark as a high-ranking member of a San Francisco syndicate.

But six months ago, around the time she showed up in New York? Nada.

It was like she'd dropped off the face of the earth when she'd joined Grimclaw's lair.

So it fit that Lark was playing me. Like my mama used to say, leopards don't change their spots.

But...this show she was putting on seemed fake. I'd stake my life that Lark was lying—that everything she'd said since I'd walked into the cell was a lie.

She needed my help, dammit, but was too stubborn—or proud—to ask me for it.

Lark released a ragged breath. "Just go, Spider," she told me. "Don't make this something it's not."

"Shut up." I backed her into a corner. "Just shut up, will you?"

Her mouth opened in outrage but her gaze flicked past me.

I gently gripped her face and gave her a soft kiss, mindful of her hurt mouth, before she said something we'd both regret. She pressed her lips together, refusing to kiss me back, and when I released her, glared at me like I was the bad guy.

"Don't..." She wiped a hand across her mouth like I'd left a bad taste. "Don't make me hate you."

I eyed her, feeling at a loss. Why couldn't I get through to her?

There. That flicker again as she looked over my shoulder like someone else was in the cell with us.

The dots connected like a string of Halloween lights.

Troll.

He could've circled back in the shadows and darted inside. Jacko and Zayne had left the Cavern door open when they'd rushed to my aid.

And here I'd been wasting time trying to have a heart-to-heart with Lark.

I swung around, pushing Lark behind me so Troll—or whoever the fuck it was—would have to go through me first, and pulled my dagger from its holster. "Show yourself, you motherfucker."

Behind me Lark made a small, agonized sound. "Spider..."

"Tell me someone's not in here," I snapped back. "Tell me I'm wrong."

"Nobody's—" Her hand touched my back. "Be...careful," she whispered. And even softer, "I'm so sick of the lies."

Troll dropped out of the shadows—and staggered. He slumped against a wall, a hand to his injury, clearly out of juice.

I stalked toward him, not even caring if he might have valuable information. I just wanted to end him. The gods knew what he'd said to Lark before I arrived, but I'd bet a year's tributes that he'd threatened her in some way.

Troll held up his hand, breath sawing in and out. "Wait," he rasped. "We can split the money, okay? A million for you and a million for me. But stake me and you won't see a penny."

Two million?

"Alright," I told him. "I'll bite. What money?"

He glanced from me to Lark.

"Don't worry about the bitch," I told him. "I can handle her. And if she's got my lair in the middle of some shit, I wanna know."

Behind me, Lark made a small sound of disbelief, like she really thought I'd sell her out to Troll. The woman still didn't trust me. But I suppose I deserved that, because I hadn't trusted her fully, either.

Troll didn't seem completely convinced, so I encouraged him with a jab of my dagger. "Talk or I'll forget why I didn't stake you as soon as you dropped out of the shadows."

"A syndicate out West. Some dude is jonesing for her."

"Let me guess—his last name is Darkman?"

Troll jerked a shoulder.

"That's what I thought," I said.

"You *knew*?" Lark whispered.

"A guess," I returned. "Your parents bought it in Vegas, the Darkmans' town, right? Go on," I told Troll. "So there's a hit on Lark?"

He shook his head, clearly exhausted. "Not a hit. They want her alive. The heir—Jared."

I nodded, starting to get the picture. Jared Darkman wanted Lark as his plaything, and apparently, she'd objected.

"He's here in the city?"

Troll's chest jerked. He tried to straighten but couldn't

manage it. "That's all I'm sayin' for now. But you need me, understand? They'll only talk to me."

"He's here," Lark muttered.

I grunted agreement. She'd escaped Jared once. He'd want to make sure it didn't happen a second time.

I studied Troll. "He's the one who split your lip?" I asked Lark.

"Yeah."

"And he's also the reason why you were sleeping outside the lair."

It wasn't a question, but Troll's start of surprise told me I was right.

"Yeah," she said lowly. She was right behind me now.

Troll shifted from one foot to the other. "You gonna believe that bitch over me?"

Darkness edged my vision. My knuckles whitened on the dagger.

Lark touched my back. "Hey. I'm outta there now."

I shook her off to get in Troll's face. "You treated her like shit," I said, my voice harsh with fury, "when you had her in your lair. And now you think you can come into my lair and smack her around? A woman under my protection?"

He raised his hands, palms out. "I'm sorry, bro. I didn't know."

"I'm not your goddamned brother, and you did know. You were Grimclaw's fucking lieutenant. And you're the same lying piece of shit as he is."

My hand flashed forward and for the second time that night, I staked a member of Grimclaw's lair. He arched his back, his agonized groan filling the small cell, and scrabbled desperately at the dagger. His stunned gaze met mine.

"You...need me."

I snorted. "I think I can find the Darkmans without your

help. And by the way," I said as I jerked the dagger back out. "I staked Grimclaw, too. You're the new alpha. Congratulations."

He fell to his ass, blood and smoke spurting from his chest. "Fuck. You."

"Get on your knees and warm me up first."

Behind me, Lark stifled a giggle, which almost made the whole night worth it.

I found a clean patch on Troll's T-shirt to wipe off my dagger with, then shoved his smoking body out of the way with my booted foot.

"You." I jerked my chin at Lark. "Come with me."

18

———————

LARK

Spider grabbed my wrist and hustled me through the gritty tunnels. I went meekly, in shock about Grimclaw and Troll. It was like the ground had been pulled out from under me, leaving me dangling in mid-air, struggling to find my footing.

I glanced at Spider's set face. Even though something was clearly bothering him, his grip was firm and reassuring. A life-line, in fact.

I turned my hand so my fingers were intertwined through his. "Thank you," I said in a gruff voice. I cleared my throat and tried again. "I—Troll was going to... The bastard said he wanted to 'see what the fuss was about.' I held him off as long as I could, but he was too strong..."

"You're all right?" Spider asked, tight-jawed.

"Yeah. You got there just in time."

For some reason, that seemed to make him angrier. He swore under his breath and flashed me a furious look, his eyes touched with his vampire. "You should've told me about Darkman."

I lifted a shoulder, let it drop. "I figured it wasn't your problem."

His expression darkened further. "I'm your alpha. If some asshole is gunning for you, I need to know."

"You keep saying that. But we both know it's not true."

I tried to pull my hand free, but he just tightened his grip. "I wouldn't piss me off if I were you."

"Yeah?" Maybe it was partly reaction, but I was starting to get angry, too. "Well, you're not making any sense. You told me not to fall in love with you. Why the fuck would I think you'd care about me and Jared Darkman?"

That made his step hitch. He rounded on me. "Damn you, Lark. You didn't even ask."

I blinked at the raw hurt on his face. "Ask what?"

He growled. "For *help*."

"But—"

"I'm a powerful man." He started off again, pulling me along with him. "I have connections. People who owe me favors. You think I'm scared of some dickhead syndicate princeling? But even when I straight out asked you, you wouldn't give me a name."

"You don't know him. He's got connections, too. I didn't want him to hurt y—" I trailed off at his livid expression.

"You were protecting *me*?" A vein throbbed visibly on his temple.

"Yeah. What's wrong with that? I lose you, I don't get paid." That was a low blow, but I was angry now, too.

He stopped and took hold of my shoulders. "So you're gonna double down on that shit? Even without those asses threatening you, you're still trying to convince me it's just business?"

I shoved him full in the chest. Infuriatingly, he barely moved.

"Fine," I snapped. "It was more. I lo—*like* you, you ass. And

I like your lair—they're good people. I didn't want them hurt because of me. You don't know what a vindictive fuck Jared can be."

"Let him try." Spider bared his fangs. "I'll make his life a living nightmare. This way."

He steered me down a narrow passage and into what appeared to be an old bank vault, complete with an 18-inch-thick reinforced concrete door. Matte-black metal boxes lined the shelves, circling a sleek gray industrial desk and a couple of rolling chairs.

Shady, a slender, dark-haired vampire I'd only met once, snapped the lid shut on one of the boxes and slid it back on a shelf, but not before I caught a glimpse of the crisp stacks of bills inside. An oil painting leaned against a shelf, and beside the laptop on the desk was a rustic wood bowl holding a fistful of uncut diamonds.

I momentarily forgot my turmoil as I took it in. "What is this?" I asked Spider.

"My office."

"You have an office?"

"Yeah." He nodded at Shady. "Leave. You can finish later."

The other vampire sent me a curious look and silently obeyed.

For a few seconds, Spider and I just stared at each other. I gulped a breath, as a cavalcade of emotions slammed into me— relief, anger, a guilty sense of freedom. Troll could burn in Hades for all I cared, but Grim had been my last relative. Maybe I should be sad, but I wasn't. Grim had sucked as both an alpha and a cousin. There was no denying the sheer weight of his constant threats and manipulations. With him gone, it felt like a heavy, suffocating blanket had been lifted off my shoulders.

Grim would've always been there in the background, threatening me with exposure. He would've drained me dry. And when he couldn't get any more from me, he would've sold me out to Jared without a second thought.

I heaved a breath. "Maybe I should've told you about Jared," I told Spider. "But I didn't wanna drag you into my mess. You've been good to me—better than I expected. This—this time with your lair has been the best. The. Best. You and your people— you don't know how freakin' awesome you are. I thought the best thing I could do for everyone was keep quiet."

Some of Spider's tension eased. "And you didn't trust me."

"Not completely," I admitted. "I had to be careful, you know? But I would've told you eventually."

He lifted a dark brow.

I lifted a shoulder, let it drop. "Probably."

He ran his hands up and down my upper arms. The adrenaline had worn off, and tiny trembles were hitting me. He frowned as I gave a shiver.

"You're shaking."

Velma slipped through the doorway, pale but looking better. "I hear you had some trouble with Troll."

"I thought you were resting," Spider grumbled, still caressing me.

She touched her bandaged shoulder. "I'm better, and I figured I should be here for this."

Spider just shook his head. "Sit down, at least." He nudged a chair toward her with his foot. "You, too," he told me.

I sank into the chair next to Velma's. Spider produced a bottle of blood-whiskey and passed me a double shot. "Drink this. You need blood."

I accepted it gratefully, wrapping my trembling hands around it. I drained it in two gulps, relishing the burn of the alcohol and blood.

Spider took the glass. "Want another?"

I shook my head as the burn spread through me, warm and

with that special energy blood imparts. The shaking was already easing.

Spider took the chair behind the desk. "Now," he said, "tell us what happened in Vegas."

"Before I do, there's something you should know." I glanced from him to Velma. "Both of you. Troll told me that someone on the inside is feeding intel to Jared Darkman."

They exchanged a look. "Did he say anything else?" Velma asked.

"No." I bit my lower lip. "I don't even know if it's a man or a woman. But I think he was telling the truth."

Velma pursed her mouth. "It tracks. We've wondered ourselves if we have a snitch. If you think of anything else, let us know, alright?"

"I will." I hesitated because who likes to be a snitch, but DeeDee made me uneasy. "Have you looked into DeeDee? She's the newest member of your lair, right?"

A line formed between Velma's black brows. "She checked out clean. I know she's jealous of you—she has a thing for Spider—but other than that, she's been a good fit for us."

"It's just a feeling. Maybe it's just that she's jealous, but it's felt like she's been gunning for me since Day One."

Spider rubbed his lower lip. "I can tell her to back off."

I winced. "No—that's okay. Just keep an open mind about her, okay? Something's off about her."

"We'll dig a little deeper," Velma promised, and I had to be satisfied with that.

"So." Spider leaned back in the chair and eyed me. "How did you end up in Darkman's sights?"

I blew out a breath. Embarrassed and a little humiliated at what it said about my family, but Spider and Velma needed to know the truth if we were going to solve this.

"Because my parents couldn't resist easy money. Jared made

it clear he was interested in me, and I played along because he would've made Las Vegas too hot for us if I hadn't."

"What a dick," Velma muttered.

Spider nodded, a muscle in the side of his jaw jumping.

My laugh held zero humor. "He is. A rich, thinks-he-can-have-any-toy-he-wants dick. But nothing happened. We danced a few times, we flirted—that's all. But he started acting all possessive, like I was already his. I told my parents that he was bad news, that we needed to leave before things blew up in our faces."

"So why the fuck does he think you owe him?" asked Spider.

"Because," I said, knowing I sounded bitter but not really caring, "behind my back, my mom and dad sold me to him. They signed a fucking contract with him. I found out just in time, and told them I'd had it. Then I got the hell out of there. They...didn't." My voice broke. I swallowed and kept going. "But I didn't know he was coming that night—I swear I didn't. It all happened so fast."

Velma whistled. Spider cursed.

The last part burst from my lips. I'd been holding it in so long it was a relief to have it out. "Maybe if I'd stayed, they'd still be alive."

"Fuck that." Spider straightened in the armchair. "They knew they were taking a risk. You're not gonna tell me that's the only job that ever went south."

"No. But it's the first time I told them no way, that I wasn't gonna be a part of it."

"You weren't allowed to say no?"

I moved a shoulder. "Yeah, I guess. But it was too late by then. They went behind my back. They said they never meant for me to go through with it—the plan was to take Jared's money and disappear."

My stomach tightened. The familiar shame gnawed at my insides—that I'd left my parents to face Jared on their own.

"So they did this behind your back."

I grimaced. "Yeah. I found Dad practically salivating over the briefcase of cash he'd gotten for me."

"Sweet Kali," muttered Velma.

Spider's handsome face was dark, but he kept up with his patient questions. "And you were what, twenty-three? Twenty-four?

"Twenty-four."

He cursed. "So you were a fucking adult—they should've gotten your agreement before signing any contracts with Darkman. You're not the one who should feel guilty."

I swallowed over a golf-ball-sized lump. "But I do. I told them I was outta there, and booked it. I would've got in touch when I cooled down, but it was too late."

"Look at me, Lark." When I did, he said, "Your parents did this to themselves. If you would've stayed, Darkman would've gotten his hands on you, too. You owe them nothing."

"I guess." I squirmed on the chair. "They weren't bad people, just...blinded by dollar signs. They really thought they could get away with it. They never meant for me to honor the contract."

Velma's mouth turned down. "They should've never put you in that situation. *Never*."

I rubbed my hands down my face. "I know. But I should've made them come with me. I should've convinced them somehow."

Spider crouched in front of me. "They made their choice when they signed that contract, Lark. They knew they were taking a risk. And they loved you, right?"

"Yeah." I dragged my teeth over my lower lip, remembering how my father had always had a joke ready, and how my mom had been such a patient teacher, making sure I could do anything from hustling pool to speaking perfect Spanish.

"So think about it—would they want you blaming yourself like this?"

I stared at Spider, at the concern for me etched in every line of his powerful, rangy body, and something inside me shifted. He was right. My parents had preached life-is-too-short-for-regrets like it was their gospel. They'd learned from their mistakes, applied the lessons to the next job.

"No," I said slowly, "they wouldn't have. They always said guilt was a waste of energy and brain power. They would've hated knowing that I was still angry and hurting and blaming myself that they'd gotten staked. In fact, Dad would've told me to stop whining and get back on the goddamn horse."

"That's what I thought," said Spider. "Not that I knew them, but I've seen you in action, and that Lark doesn't give up. If she can't fight her way out of trouble, she charms her way out of it. I figure you got that from them."

Beside me, Velma nodded.

"I suppose." My mouth twitched up. "Hell, they were even more charming. They'd had a hundred-plus years to work on their game."

"Yeah?" He gave a small smile in return. "I mean, what they did was fucked up, but they sound like a helluva pair."

"They were." I reached for his hands. "Thank you. They would've liked you." I gave a lopsided grin, trying to lighten things up because if I didn't, I was going to get all sentimental. "Especially your money."

Spider squeezed my hands, his brown eyes warm. "Damn, I hate to think about you being all alone. But no more, understand? You're one of us now. You tell me you were just trying to put Grimclaw off, then I believe you. Hell, I should've realized that's what you were doing, so that's on me. It won't happen again. Okay?"

"Okay." I looked at his long, competent fingers wrapped around mine, blinking back tears. He'd accepted my explanation completely, and he was offering me his trust. He couldn't know what that meant.

"So," Spider prompted. "You're officially a member of the Cavern now. Right?"

He said it with typical alpha confidence, but the fact that he was pressing me on it told me he wanted the words from me. The next move was mine. I was free to do whatever I wanted. I could run again, or I could stand and fight.

I drew a deep breath, equal parts scared and exhilarated.

The future was a wild card, but for the first time ever, it was mine to deal. I had a shot to rebuild, to seize control of my life, with Spider and his motley crew of misfits backing me up. There wasn't any other group I'd rather roll with.

"Yes." I squeezed Spider's fingers and let some of what I was feeling onto my face in smile that felt too big for my face. "I'd be honored to join your lair."

"Permanently?"

"Permanently," I confirmed.

That raw something flashed in his eyes. "You won't be sorry," he said so fiercely, it sounded like a vow.

I held his gaze, my heart thumping at the intensity emanating from him. Maybe he was feeling some of what I did, too?

I leaned closer, drawn to him like he was a human magnet.

His Adam's apple bobbed. "Lark...?"

"Welcome to the Cavern," Velma said, and we both jolted. "Yeah," she murmured dryly, "I'm still here." She chuckled.

"Okay." Spider rose from his crouch and retook his seat, leaving me to wonder what he'd been about to ask. "Lark, why don't you start by telling us everything you know about Jared Darkman."

"I can do better than that." I was on my feet now, mind

working. "I know Jared—how to push his fucking buttons. Let's turn this around on him."

Velma nodded approvingly. "I like how you think."

"Thanks." I grinned at her. "Jared's already made one mistake—following me to New York. It's not his town now, is it?"

Spider straightened in his chair. "No, it's not. It's the Krals'."

"And you have an 'in' with them," I pointed out, an idea taking shape.

"So I do..."

Our gazes locked, and somehow I knew his mind was working along the same lines as mine.

"Talk," he told me. "I'm not making any promises, understand? But I wanna hear more."

19

SPIDER

"This is so Goth." Beneath her lacy, wine-colored mask, Lark's heavily mascaraed eyes roved approvingly around the cavernous chamber. "I like."

My own mask dangled from my hand. I followed her gaze to the iron chandelier studded with blood-red candles, and then to the deep purple roses twined with ivy creeping up the marble columns and over the bannisters.

"And this is just the entrance," I murmured.

The Kral primus and his mate went all out for the Midnight Masquerade, throwing it in a massive subterranean hall. Music drifted up the stairs to where we waited to show our invitation —hand-crafted paper with a wax seal bearing the Kral wolf—to the pair of guards flanking the colossal iron doors.

Behind us, a crew of vampires and thralls got into line. The vampires, all top-tier syndicate players, oozed dominance. My own dominance flared in response. I grabbed Lark's gloved hand and looped it through my arm, making it clear she was off limits.

Lark cast me a questioning glance but closed her fingers

around the sleeve of my tux. I'd gone with a monochrome look tonight—black tux, matching shirt, a skinny black tie tucked into my satin vest. My lucky dagger was in a special pocket of the vest. If all went well, it would end the night in Jared Darkman's heart.

"Mom would've killed for an invitation to this," said Lark. "If only..." She bit her lower lip. "Sorry."

"Don't be sorry. You miss them. I get it."

In the two weeks since Lark had officially joined the lair, we'd spent nearly every spare minute together. I'd even started including her in my briefings with Velma and the rest of my top people. Her parents might've been selfish dicks, but they'd done a good job educating her. She was creative and quick-thinking, with this innate ability to adapt and innovate on the spot, and a knack for seeing things from angles most people missed.

Her presence brought a new energy to our group, challenging us to think differently and push the boundaries of our strategies. It was more than just her intelligence, though. Lark had a natural magnetism that drew people in. Her confidence and determination were infectious, inspiring those around her to rise to the occasion. She was fast becoming an indispensable part of my inner crew.

"I do." She rested her head against my shoulder. "But I'm also angry at them. I know I should let it go, but...." She expelled a breath.

"I know." I brushed my lips over her temple. That story she'd told about being "sold" to Jared Darkman still gave me chills. In my opinion, her folks had got what was coming to them. "But this is where you get your revenge, right?"

I hated even putting Lark in the same ballroom as Darkman, but we hadn't been able to determine who in the lair was betraying us. (If, that is, Troll had told Lark the truth about someone feeding Darkman intel.) And her plan was solid—better than anything I'd come up with. If I wanted Darkman permanently out of the picture, this was our best option.

"True." She brightened and lifted her head, the ruby-and-diamond encrusted gold hoops I'd given her earlier catching the candlelight. "And if Mom and Dad were here, they probably would've had me lifting that big-ass emerald on your finger."

We both looked at my index finger. I snorted.

Lark chuckled...and something in me preened at knowing I'd cheered her up.

We reached the front of the line. One of the guards took our invitation, checking our names against a list. Lark got a second glance, his eyes lingering on the smooth skin exposed by the cutout over her breasts.

I growled lowly, and he swallowed and waved us through the doors. "Enjoy your evening, Sir. Madam."

"Thank you," Lark said with a regal nod.

With her hair up in a sleek black twist and a bored smile on her lips, she fit in with the other guests in a way I never would. Not that I gave a rat's ass about fitting in. As far as I was concerned, the syndicates could shove their rules and hierarchies where the sun don't shine.

But Lark was different. She was in her element, moving to the top of the wide marble staircase with a grace and ease that drew admiring glances. Commanding attention even among the vampire elite.

When this was over, a good man would pull some strings, help her escape my world. Someone with Lark's looks, self-possession and chameleon-like ability to blend in anywhere from the Underworld to a posh ball could rake in serious cash selling her skills to the highest bidder.

Too bad I wasn't a good man.

Because I'd made up my mind to keep Lark. In a few short

weeks, she'd become necessary to me. She was Amina and then some—sharp, fearless, adaptable.

Velma was right. I'd spent too long stuck in a limbo, punishing myself for Amina's death. Afraid to let another woman break the chains around my heart in case I lost her, too.

But Lark had changed everything, and the thought of going back to the way things were made my chest compress like a giant vise had me in its grip.

For the first time in years, I felt something real—happiness, hope.

Mine. My vampire—the primal part of me—had seen the truth before I had, and I was damned if I'd let Lark go now. She was my mate, and as soon as we were free of the Darkman asshole, I was going to tell her that. Hell, if she'd just agree to the fucking bond, I'd promise her the moon and stars.

"Ready?" I asked her, adjusting the mesh mask on my face. Damn thing was too tight—a new design of DeeDee's—but for now I was stuck with it.

Lark lifted her chin, determination etched in every line of her beautiful body. "Let's do this."

We started down wide marble stairs flanked by ebony rails carved with wolves on the prowl, their teeth bared, tails supporting the railing. The ballroom below was filled with masked, shadowy figures; men in dark tuxedos and topcoats, women draped in sultry fall colors—reds, oranges, golds. A fog machine spewed mist that hugged the floor and slithered beneath the towering Gothic arches.

At the bottom of the stairs, Lark sent a sweeping glance around. "I don't see him."

"He's here," I said. "Or he will be. Remember, whatever happens, I've got your back. Velma and Monster, too." Velma was against the wall, standing at attention in a black Kral uniform, and Monster was stationed near the restrooms.

Lark kissed my cheek. "Thank you."

After this night, I'd owe Zaq Kral, big time. He'd not only talked his primus father into letting us trap Jared Darkman at the Midnight Masquerade, he'd allowed me to insert two of my top people into tonight's security detail.

A server in a black corset and red skirt approached, a tray of blood-champagne balanced on her palm.

"Want a drink?" I asked Lark, but she shook her head.

"Let's dance, okay? Maybe we'll be able to see him."

The band was playing a slow, ponderous waltz, and the floor was packed. I'd never met a supernatural who was a bad dancer—we love music and moving to a beat. But dancing with Lark was like dancing with a fairy. Light and airy, she easily matched my every move.

"Of course, you're an expert at ballroom dancing," I said wryly.

She tipped her head. "That a problem?"

"No. We're just different, you and me."

But I'm still keeping you.

I spun us around, navigating through the swirl of masked men and women. Lark flung back her head, the skirt's red-and-purple pleats flaring out around her toned thighs.

"You're a good dancer, too. And I like how we're different." Her lips curved in a slow, sexy smile.

I moved my hand lower on her back, slipping it through the diamond cutout. Her muscles flexed beneath my touch. I spread my fingers, caressing her at that sensitive spot just above her ass, and sure enough, she gave that small shiver I loved.

The band switched to a salsa. I gathered Lark closer until her lower body was basically glued to mine. We stepped forward and backward, hips swinging with the beat. I glanced down, eating up her cleavage with my eyes. Promising myself that at the end of the night, I would lick a trail from the bottom of that peek-a-boo diamond to the top.

And then I would slice through that collar of material around her pretty throat and sink my fangs into her...

She slanted me a mock-glare from beneath her long lashes. "Focus, Spider-Dude."

"Then stop flashing your tits at me."

She arched her back, giving me a better view. "But it's so fun."

I slapped her ass. "You are so bad."

Her grin was an arrow to my heart. Pain and pleasure all wrapped up in a complicated ball.

There was a stir at entrance. Zaq Kral had arrived, along with his mate and Jared Darkman. Darkman studied the crowd with cold blue eyes, looking as spoiled and arrogant in person as he had in his social media feeds (yeah, the dude posted about himself, usually shirtless).

A dark smile tipped up my lips. He'd taken the bait.

The Krals had extended Darkman an invite—they'd known he was in New York, because he'd had to ask permission to enter their territory. And we'd spread a rumor that I was bringing Lark to the Midnight Masquerade, assuming it would reach his ears.

"He's here," Lark said in an undertone. Beneath my hands, she vibrated like a plucked string but kept dancing.

"Breathe, baby," I said, and her lungs emptied.

The Vegas vampire tossed his shoulder-length brown curls in a practiced move and held out his hand to Zaq's long-legged blond mate, inviting her to dance. She exchanged a look with Zaq, then gave curt nod, and the two moved onto the dance floor.

"He's dancing with Zaq Kral's mate," I said. "Princess Renata."

Lark wrapped her hands around my neck. Right before my eyes, she straightened her spine and morphed into a bored party girl again.

"He's looking for me," she whispered.

My grip on her tightened. "He's not going to touch you. That's a fucking promise."

I'd lost Amina. I'd stab a stake into my own heart before I'd lose Lark.

20

LARK

The band launched into another salsa tune, the rhythm pulsing in my body. I pressed against Spider, feeling the heat between us, and swiveled my hips in sync with the beat. Focusing on the music and the glittery feeling of being out with this strong, sexy man.

When Jared Darkman arrived, terror had zoomed over me, jamming my lungs. I'd trembled like a freaking rabbit. And Spider had known, had said exactly the right thing. That he was facing this with me made me so damn grateful.

His dark eyes caught mine. "You good?"

My chest loosened. I drew a steadying inhale. "Yeah."

His sculpted lips tilted up. "That's my Lark."

He wrapped his arms around me, pulling me even closer. Adrenaline fizzed in me. Spider's hand was inside the back of my dress again, his middle finger sliding between my ass cheeks to my thong, causing a needy tug low in my belly.

He rubbed his hips against me, letting me feel how hard he was beneath his tuxedo pants. "When this is over," he said in husky tones, "you're so going to get fucked."

I let my mouth curve in a teasing smile. "Promise?"

Yeah, I realized he was trying to distract me. But he was also reminding me of the endgame: turn the tables on Jared Darkman and come out of this alive and free.

Please let me come out of this alive and free.

Because I wanted to have sex with Spider after this was over. And then again tomorrow night and the night after that.

But I wanted more than that. I wanted to dig into what made him tick, find out the little things like his favorite color and how he met Velma. I craved the big stuff too. I wanted to hear the story of how he rose to be the Underworld kingpin... and if he could ever love me like he loved Amina.

Spider's spine went rigid beneath my hands. "Don't look, but he's to your right. Five yards or so away."

I pulled back my shoulders. "He recognized me?"

"Think so. He keeps trying to see your face."

The salsa finished, and Spider steered me off the dance floor, a hand on the small of my back. He snagged a couple of champagne glasses from a server and handed me one.

"He's still dancing with Zaq's mate," he said out of the side of his mouth.

Sipping my champagne, I turned and faced the dance floor. "I see him."

Jared Darkman in the flesh, his hard body dressed in a bespoke tux. And yeah, I was still afraid, but even stronger was my stone-cold determination to end this.

No more hiding in the Underworld for me.

First, we'd take care of Jared Darkman. And then I'd charm the ever livin' hell out of Spider the Underworld Kingpin until he couldn't help but fall in love with me.

Spider's arm pressed against mine and I flashed him a quick, I've-got-this smile.

He winked back. *I know.*

I glanced at Princess Renata. She was lean and wiry, with big gray eyes and a heart-shaped face. But what caught my attention was her complete lack of interest in Jared and his brooding, Lord Byron vibe. He whispered something in her ear, and she shot back a reply that made him flinch and put a good half foot of space between them.

I fought the urge to laugh.

That glittery feeling hit me again—the kind you get just before pulling off a heist. Sure, we might not have plotted every detail like my parents would've, but the plan was solid.

Bait Jared into trying to snatch me, then send an alert via the tracking device I wore. Spider would burst in along with Zaq Kral, catching him in the act. As an out-of-town guest, Jared would have broken one of the most basic rules of syndicate hospitality: Don't mess with another vampire's lover.

When Spider staked him, not even Jared's father could object. And if Darkman Senior had a problem, he could take it up with Karoly Kral—one of the world's most powerful primuses.

"Alright," I said. "Let's do this."

Spider's eyes flicked to my elbow-length black gloves. "You got your blade?"

"Yep." The skinny silver blade was firmly in its slot on my inner left forearm, a bit of insurance Spider had insisted I bring. "And the tracking device is activated." I touched the lower point of the diamond cutout where I'd sewn a tiny bead that would alert Spider. If something went wrong, it was also a GPS device that he and Velma could track on their phones.

I blew a kiss to Spider and slid along the edge of the dance floor, heading for the restrooms. He set off in the opposite direction, searching for a quiet corner to fade into the shadows and follow me.

The restroom stalls were like mini bathrooms with their

own sinks, mirrors, and personal care products, and toilets with built-in bidets. This early in the evening, all five stalls were empty.

Perfect. Jared wasn't an idiot—he wouldn't try and kidnap me if anyone else was around.

I ducked into a stall to smooth my skirt and adjusted my mask—not DeeDee's handmade mask, either. I'd worn that into the limo but switched to a mask I'd found in Spider's closet instead.

Velma and Monster hadn't been able to turn up anything off about DeeDee, but she'd gone back to being fake-nice. Call me paranoid, but her eagerness for me to wear her mask had set off a giant red light flashing in my brain. Plus, the mask had been itchy and a little too heavy.

Footsteps sounded. I stilled, my hands fisting, until I heard the *tap-tap* of high heels.

Not Jared, then.

I tapped the glove over the silver blade for luck and exited the stall. A masked woman in a party dress blocked my way.

When I tried to go around her, she glowered at me from beneath her straight black fringe. "Where's my mask?"

I reared back. "DeeDee?"

"Yeah. Where's the mask I made you?"

What the fuck? I veered around her, aiming for the exit. "I like this one better."

"Jesus. I don't know why Jared wants you so bad," she muttered, and struck out at my stomach with a silver switchblade.

She almost caught me—I hadn't expected an attack, and I was still stuck on that "Jared." But she was a human and five times slower than me. I jumped back, body curved like a C, and the blade just missed me.

Shaking off my surprise, I snapped into action, using her

own momentum to shove her headfirst into the stall and onto her knees in front of the toilet.

Slamming the toilet seat up, I pushed her face toward the bowl of water. "What do you know about Jared Darkman?"

"Go to Hades, bitch."

"Wrong answer." I dunked her in the toilet bowl, holding her down while I counted—slowly—to ten. Then I pulled her out. "Now," I said grimly as she came up retching, "what do you know about Jared Darkman?"

She wiped the water from her face. "He'll kill me," she whined.

"Yeah?" I pressed her head downward again, stopping just above the water line. "But if you don't talk, you'll die right now."

"No!" She twisted against my grip but couldn't break free. "I'll talk, I'll talk."

"Smart choice. What did the mask have to do with it?"

"You don't know? I thought that's why you aren't wearing it."

"Because—?"

"I wove silver thread through it."

I knit my brows. "I didn't see any silver."

"Because I'm good. Those masks make me a lot of money on the Dark Web. Way more than I can make bartending."

"So why are you working for Jared Darkman?"

"He's paying a lot of money for you. And I don't like you."

I shook my head. "Gods, you're an ass. What are you going to do when Spider finds out? You're not gonna live to see any of that money. You'll be at the bottom of the Hudson River."

She gave a weird little shrug, like she didn't care. That's when it hit me—she'd crafted Spider's mask, too.

A chill shot down my spine. Silver is a vampire's Achilles' heel. Spider was powerful, but silver could still bring him to his knees. Already, it could have entered his bloodstream, weakening him...leaving him vulnerable. I had to warn him.

"You bitch—" I smashed her forehead against the toilet's

porcelain rim, leaving her groaning on the floor, her hand to her bleeding head.

I burst out of the stall just as Velma slammed into the restroom. My gaze shot to hers, my heart drumming in my ears.

"Where's Spider?" we demanded in unison.

21

SPIDER

The first wave of dizziness hit me as I passed a large stone wolf with glowing red eyes.

Vampires don't get sick. Dragging off my tie, I shoved it into my pocket, loosened the first couple of buttons of my shirt, and kept going.

Why in Hades was my mask so uncomfortable? I readjusted the black mesh over my upper face. The rough fabric scraped against my skin. DeeDee's new design needed serious work.

Two hard-faced vampires closed in, their gleaming eyes cold and unfeeling. They herded me out a side door into a dimly lit corridor. It stretched before me, endless as a nightmare, the flickering lights casting eerie shadows on the walls.

A second wave of dizziness blurred my vision. My stomach heaved, and bile pressed into my throat. I pressed a hand to my mouth and managed not to vomit up the blood-champagne I'd just drunk.

Each step felt like a struggle, the oppressive atmosphere pressing down on me as I fought to stay upright.

A dull nudge from my brain. *Silver poisoning.*

Had the champagne been spiked with colloidal silver?

And why was my face on fire? I clawed at the mask.

"Don't let him take that off," the guy to my left barked.

They grabbed my arms, pulling my hands away from my face.

That's when it hit me—the silver was in the mask. The one DeeDee had made to match Lark's, although Lark hadn't liked hers, and had changed to another in the limo.

Lark.

Terror iced my gut. What if Lark had been right and DeeDee was the snitch, the person leaking intel to Darkman? And DeeDee knew what Lark was wearing. No wonder the snake had made Lark in the ballroom so quickly.

A surge of fear allowed me to throw the men off me. I tore the silver-laced mesh from my face and flung it away.

"Forget the mask," the dude on my right snapped. "You take him down. I'll drag him into the shadows."

I broke into a run—or tried to. It felt like my feet belonged to someone else.

The other guy tackled me, slamming me to the marble floor. Pain radiated through me as I struggled to push him off. He pinned me down, his weight pressing me into the cold marble, the metallic taste of blood filling my mouth. My vision blurred again, but I grimly forced myself to focus.

I had to fight for Lark's sake.

And where was Zaq? He'd sworn he'd have my back, and if I trusted any syndicate man, it was him.

Both vampires were on me now. I bucked against their holds.

I couldn't lose Lark. Amina's loss had been bad, but losing Lark would break me.

I had thirty seconds, tops, to break free before they pulled me into the shadows. I fought like a beast.

Without the silver sucking at my strength, I was stronger. I jerked free of first one, then the other, and went for my lucky dagger. But the poison slowed me enough that one of them grabbed me and got me in a chokehold before I could pull it from my vest.

He squeezed my windpipe like a boa constrictor, using his free hand against the forearm around my neck to apply a pressure that would've killed a human. Me, he couldn't kill—not like this—but he could make me lose consciousness and then pull me into the shadows.

And he was winning...

A wave of dread swamped me. All I could think of was Lark and what that fucking princeling would do to her if I didn't escape.

I slammed my elbow into his groin. He let out a vicious curse, but momentarily loosened his grip on me. Breaking out of the chokehold, I threw him off me and pushed myself up on my hands and knees, sucking oxygen.

I caught a flash of silver and threw myself to the side, scrabbling for my own weapon. An inhuman hiss, and then one of the vampires landed near my head, eyes glassy, a blade sticking out of his chest. From the corner of my eye, I saw the other fall to the floor. He'd been staked as well.

What the—?

A hand landed on my back, and I snarled and swung around into a crouch, my dagger in my hand.

Zaq Kral stood over me. He lifted both hands in surrender. "Chill, man. It's only me and Renata."

He nodded at his mate, who'd pulled the blade from one of the men and was calmly wiping it off with a handful of cocktail napkins. I'd heard a rumor that Renata used to be a slayer but hadn't believed it. Now, I believed.

"Lark," I croaked, and dragged out my phone. It was dead, cracked almost in two from when I must've landed top of it. "No!"

I cursed, more afraid than I could ever remember being.

"You can't track her?" Zaq said as Renata cleaned the second blade as well and handed it to Zaq.

I shook my head and surged to my feet. "No. But Velma can. Where's Darkman?"

Renata's lip curled. She tossed the bloody napkins on the smoking remains of my attackers and answered, "Dancing."

"That was five or ten minutes ago," said Zaq. "We followed you per the plan. But Velma and Monster have eyes on Lark, right?"

I gave a jerky nod. "Call Velma for me—ASAP. Tell her my phone is broken, that we need her to track Lark."

Renata already had her phone out. "On it."

I didn't question how she had Velma's number, just took off for the restrooms, shoving people aside in my hurry. I probably would've started a mini war if Zaq hadn't stayed with me, ordering the gaping crowd to let me through.

I busted through the restroom door, Zaq on my heels. In an open stall, a blond vampire in a red gown knelt over a semiconscious DeeDee, about to sink her fangs into the human's neck.

I did a doubletake. How the fuck had DeeDee gotten into the Midnight Masquerade?

But it was basically a signed confession. She was part of this, damn her.

"Get away from her," I snarled at the blonde kneeling over her.

"Mine," she hissed back, baring her fangs at me. "Find your own."

Zaq stepped forward. "You heard him—get out of the damn stall."

Her eyes widened. "My lord. This human belongs to you?"

He jerked his chin at me. "Not me. Him."

"Name's Spider," I informed her, and her brows climbed.

"The Underworld's Spider?"

"That's me. Get the fuck out of there."

Her mouth compressed, but she retracted her fangs and obeyed. I stepped past her into the stall and grabbed DeeDee around the neck.

Her gaze slid from mine. Fear and guilt oozed off her like emotional slime.

I gave her a shake. "Look into my eyes, damn you."

"Go to hell," she muttered weakly.

I brought my face close to hers and waited until she looked back at me, then slammed a compulsion into her with everything I had. "*Where's Lark?*"

"With...Jared."

"And where's that?"

"Don't know."

Despair fisted my chest. It was the truth—she couldn't lie under a compulsion. "How long ago did he take her?"

"Don't...know."

"It can't have been long," Zaq muttered. "Five minutes at the most. We can still catch her."

I nodded, even though, for a vampire, five minutes was plenty of time to have spirited Lark miles away.

"One last question," I said to DeeDee. "Are you the one feeding intel to Darkman?"

She pressed her lips together, fighting not to answer, but I was too strong for her. "Yes," she burst out. "But not about you. Just Lark."

"But Lark is mine," I told her softly, and squeezed her throat until her eyes bugged out. I thrust her away from me and stalked out of the stall. "Drain the bitch," I told the vampire in the red dress.

Renata was on her phone. "Hang on," she told the other person. To me, she said, "Velma's not answering, but security said they saw her running toward the West Side. No sign of Darkman or Lark, though."

"He must've taken her out of here in the shadows,"

said Zaq.

I rasped a curse and took off, hoping to catch them when he dropped back out of the shadows. Renata went with me, and Zaq called, "I'll grab security and meet you in front of the building."

I raised a hand in acknowledgment and picked up the pace. Together, me and Renata raced up the marble steps, through the foyer and outside to the nondescript industrial zone above the ballroom.

The only trace of Lark was a single, purply red stiletto teetering on the curb. My heart dropped into my fancy leather shoes.

I snatched up the stiletto. "Any word from Velma?"

Renata shook her head, her full lips pressed into a tight line.

Zaq and a couple of guys in tuxes burst out of the building. Instead of security, he'd brought his brothers. The three might be dhampirs, but they were stupid-powerful, and along with their father, owned this city. I felt a tinge of hope. If anyone could help me find Lark, they could.

"You see where they went?" Zaq asked.

"No." I grabbed his arm, uncaring of his older brother Gabriel's frown. "You have cams, right? You can find her. Please, Zaq."

I couldn't remember the last time I'd said 'please,' but for Lark, I'd drop to my goddamn knees and beg.

"You can't track her yourself?" asked his younger brother Rafe.

I shot him a quick, despairing look. Why were we standing here discussing this? But I answered, because I needed his help.

"My phone's busted and we don't know where Velma is."

"She was the backup," Zaq muttered.

The three brothers exchanged a look.

I released Zaq. "The cams," I urged. "I'll try Monster. Maybe he knows something."

Before I finished the sentence, the silver-haired dhampir dashed out of the building, skidding to a stop when he saw me. "Velma texted. Lark's on the West Side."

"Where?" I demanded.

"Tenth Avenue, moving north. Velma's following them—she was in the shadows, that's why she couldn't text before."

Zaq squeezed my shoulder. "Okay, now we have something. And Velma's with her. She'll be safe."

"Unless Darkman's crew gets Velma, too," muttered Rafe.

Zaq elbowed his younger brother. "Not helpful."

Gabriel had his phone out. "We need video on Tenth Avenue ASAP," he barked.

Monster glanced at his own screen. "Velma just checked in. They're heading for the heliport on West 30th."

My heart leapt. "Tell her we're on our way, to stall him if she has to. We can't let him get Lark on a helicopter."

"Forget the video," Gabriel said into his phone. "Send a half-dozen soldiers to the West 30th Heliport."

The heliport was a little over a mile away. I could cover that in under four minutes. I shot off, knowing every second counted, Zaq keeping pace with me.

With every step, I prayed we wouldn't be too late. That once again, I wouldn't fail the woman I loved.

Because yeah, I loved Lark. I felt the truth clear to my toes. My heart reached out to hers, the mate bond questing for its match.

One section of the heliport was lit up like it was noon. A shiny brown chopper was warming up on a helipad next to the Hudson, its rotors spinning slowly as the pilot prepared for takeoff. Ten yards away, Darkman had Lark pressed to his front, an arm around her throat, a knife to her chest. She was barefoot, her hair spilling out of that movie-star twist.

Only the thought that he might stake her while I watched

kept me from stalking forward and ripping his head from his body. A blood-tinged blackness edged my vision. I prowled toward them, my dagger gripped in one hand, a low, continuous growl filling my head that was nearly as loud as the engine's roar. It took me a few seconds to realize the growling was coming from me.

"Easy, bro." Zaq reached out and slapped his palm to my chest, stopping me at the edge of the circle of light. "She's fine, yeah?" he said under his breath. "We have a little time. He doesn't want to hurt her if he can avoid it—he's gone to a fuckton of trouble to get her, right?"

I swung my head to look at him, taking in what he'd said through the roaring in my brain. "Alright," I said hoarsely. "But he's mine. I want your word on that."

"Of course, man."

"Who's there?" Darkman squinted in our direction. "Come any closer and I'll stake the bitch."

"I'll talk," Zaq told me quietly. "You stay in the background."

My jaw clenched so tight my back teeth hurt. Bloody Hades, I hated feeling powerless like this. It was like Amina all over again.

But Zaq was right. Darkman was more likely to listen to him.

"Alright," I replied, "but if I see an opening, I'm gonna grab her."

"And I'll try to give you that opening." My friend sauntered forward, hands open at his sides. "Let the woman go, Jared. She's ours."

"What d'you mean, she's yours?"

"Our territory, dude. That makes the lady ours. You hurt her, you'll set off a blood feud with our syndicate. Your father isn't going to like that."

Darkman's throat worked, his eyes darting nervously around.

Lark, though, stood straight-backed and steady, the wind whipping at her skirt. Her eyes somehow found me in the darkness where I lurked. She smiled, and I felt the weight of the trust she had in me.

It left me both humbled and proud, a fierce love for her churning my insides. I just wished I had half her courage, because for the life of me, I couldn't bring myself to smile back. Not with my heart on the line. I was too gutted by the possibility of losing her.

Gabriel, Rafe and Renata raced up. I caught sight of Velma creeping in from the other side, and I knew that Monster must be around somewhere, too.

Gabriel sidled up next to me. "I got word to the pilot," he told me out of the side of his mouth. "He knows that if he takes off, he'll be dead by morning."

A wave of emotion smacked me hard. "Thanks, man," I returned gruffly. "I owe you—big time."

The tall, green-eyed prince grunted, then jerked his head at his youngest brother. "Rafe, you go with Zaq. Two-on-one will give Jared something to think about. But keep it cool, got it? We don't want to do anything to set him off."

"On it," Rafe replied with a cocky grin and strolled after his middle brother.

To me, Gabriel murmured, "We'll get your Lark back. Those two could talk a bird out of a tree."

"I hope so," I returned...and that's when it hit me that this time I wasn't powerless.

That this time, I wasn't on my own, alpha of a fledgling lair. I was powerful in my own right, and not just because I was the Underworld kingpin.

I had friends now like the Kral brothers. And I had Lark herself, strong and smart and sneaky.

My mouth curved. Jared Darkman didn't know what he'd stepped into.

22

LARK

I drank in the sight of Spider, my eyes locking onto him so that I barely registered the three men who ran up with him. He looked like he'd been in a fight. His hair was disheveled and red marks marred his brown skin in the shape of DeeDee's mesh mask.

But he was okay.

He was okay.

I'd been so afraid ever since Jared had dragged me into the shadows and out of the building, where he'd pushed me into a waiting limo. The entire ride I'd fought a raw, terrible fear that something had happened to Spider, because otherwise he'd never have let Jared take me out of the ballroom.

Jared had been agitated. He'd taunted me that my lover had been staked, and I'd died a little inside, until it hit me that Jared was lying, because I *knew* that Spider was still alive.

Now Spider's eyes burned into mine. Something passed between us and I *felt* his terror, a twin to mine. Terror, and a fierce determination.

I'm here, Lark, and I'll burn Manhattan to the fucking ground if I have to. Because I'm not losing you now.

I drew a shaky inhale. Okay, then.

Jared snarled, "Come back, damn you," and I cut my eyes to the side in time to see his bodyguards slipping away.

"No way," one muttered. "This is Kral territory. They're in charge." He jerked his head at the three dark-haired, tuxedoed men with Spider, who now that I looked closer, appeared to be a trio of Greek gods come to life.

Zaq Kral sauntered forward, followed by a guy who had to be his younger brother Rafe. And the third had to be Gabriel, the Kral crown prince.

Holy crap, the Kral Dark Angels themselves had come to my rescue. What kind of favor had Spider done Zaq, anyway?

"Look, Zaq." Jared pitched his voice to be heard about the helicopter's engine. "I don't want any trouble with you. The woman signed a contract with me."

Zaq shrugged his big shoulders, but before he could speak, Spider moved into the light.

"She didn't sign anything," he said in ringing tones. "Her parents did."

"That's right," I muttered, adding, "Without my knowledge or permission."

"Shut the fuck up," Jared growled in my ear.

I scowled but obeyed. Jared was on a hair trigger. It wouldn't take much to set him off.

"Look, dude," said Zaq. "Spider's a friend. Find another woman."

Jared stiffened. He glanced at where Spider had moved into the light. "That jumped-up Underworld lord?"

That was a mistake. Zaq's expression darkened, and Spider stiffened, his muscles hardening under the elegant tux.

"That's right," Zaq said. "Now let Lark go and maybe you walk out of here alive."

"Not so fast." Jared's fingers dug painfully into my throat. "I want a guarantee."

Rafe cut through the tension. "No problem, dude. We can work something out."

Spider eased another step forward. He looked calm, almost bored, but I was picking up his emotions like I would a human's, and he was literally vibrating with a savage, you-touched-her-now-you-die fury.

My mouth dropped open as the realization hit me. That was the mate bond I was feeling. It ran between us like a live wire, crackling with intensity.

We were mates?

So much of what had happened made sense now. The way we'd immediately connected. The constant battle not to fall head over heels for him. The way he was the most beautiful man in the world to me, even when surrounded by the Dark Angels.

His gaze held mine, and somehow, I knew that he felt it, too.

Spider's protectiveness, his need, his rage, all of it surged through me, binding us together in a way that defied logic. The world narrowed to the space between us, and I knew, without a doubt, that I was not alone in this fight, and that I wasn't fighting just for my survival, but for Spider's—and vice versa.

I stood a little taller, outwardly relaxed, but inside I was grinning like a freakin' wolf because Jared Darkman was going *down*.

Zaq and Rafe spread apart. I sensed Jared's distraction, his head turning from side to side, following them.

It was the chance I'd been waiting for. I slipped the dagger from my glove.

Neither Kral flicked an eyelid. But they knew. Zaq was talking again, soothing Jared without making any promises.

Rafe slid a hand into his front pocket. Jared jabbed the blade he'd been holding to my chest at Rafe, barking, "Keep your fucking hands where I can see them."

Abruptly, the helicopter's engine cut off. "What the fuck?" Jared shouted.

Anticipation buzzed through me, electric and fierce.

Now.

I drove my blade into his thigh with all my strength. His stifled scream echoed in my ears as I tucked my chin into my shoulder and dropped down, making a dead weight of myself.

"Bitch," Jared spat out, fighting to regain control of me. "You'll pay for that."

I twisted and turned, trying to escape his hold.

And then Zaq Kral was there, shoving me behind him with a firm hand. At the same time, Spider rushed us, his motions a blur.

Jared brought his blade up but he was too late. With lethal precision, Spider shoved his lucky dagger into my kidnapper's chest and gave a hard twist. "See you in Hades," he gritted in Jared's stunned face.

Velma skidded to a halt a few feet away as Spider jerked the blade free. Jared collapsed to the asphalt like his strings had been cut, the gaping wound in his chest spurting blood.

"Aw, damn," she said. "You get all the fun."

Spider swung around. His gaze settled on me, safely behind Zaq. His expression was feral, his irises rimmed with a blue so bright it was like a neon flashlight aimed into my heart. He dropped the dagger, letting it clatter to the pavement, and moved forward, his twists flying around his shoulders.

I launched myself at him, and he caught me in his arms, raining kisses over my face. "You're free. I was afraid we'd be too late. But you're alright. Tell me you're alright, damn it." He pulled back and leveled a furious scowl at me.

"I am. I am." Legs twined around his hips, I hugged him back, my chest rising and falling in relief. Spider was unharmed, and I was free. Jared Darkman could never bother me again. "But what about you? You're okay? I was so worried when I realized DeeDee had woven silver into your mask…"

He seemed taken aback. "You were worried for me?"

"Of course, I was. I knew Jared must've done something to you or else he'd never have gotten me out of the building."

Spider cupped my face. "I'm fine, baby. The silver slowed me down a little, that's all."

I kissed him. "And you came for me."

"Of course." He caught my gaze, held it. "I'll always come for you."

My lips trembled. "I know," I whispered.

"But just so you know," he added sternly, "you're not going anywhere. The hell with this leaving-in-a-month stuff. I'm keeping you."

A sob escaped my lips. But I was laughing, too, as I brushed a lock back from his face. "I love you, okay? I don't want to be anywhere but here."

He gave me a quick, hard kiss, then touched his forehead to mine. "Say it again."

"I don't want to be anywhere but here."

His eyes narrowed at my teasing. "Not that."

I rubbed my lips over his. "I love you," I said, enunciating each word slowly and clearly.

His breath sighed out. "Yeah, that."

Zaq cleared his throat, and we turned to look at him. Beyond him, Velma was looking on like a benevolent South Asian goddess in her pressed Kral syndicate uniform. She caught my eye and gave me a short, woman-to-woman nod.

I winked back.

"We've got a limo here," Zaq said. "You want us to send you home?"

Home? I blinked rapidly.

I guess I did have a home now.

And a family.

And Spider.

Emotion welled up in me. I got misty-eyed, even as my smile widened.

Spider shifted me in his arms so that my legs were over one of his arms, muttering something about me being barefoot. I slung an arm around his neck and swiped at my eyes.

"Hell, no," I said with a sidelong grin at my own personal Underworld kingpin. "We have something to celebrate. I wanna dance. Let's go back to the Masquerade." I kicked my nylon-clad feet. "But I'll need shoes. I think one's in Jared's limo."

"I have the other one," Spider said, and, with a flourish worthy of a Disney prince, pulled it out of his pocket and slipped it on my foot.

~

"C'MERE." Spider drew me into his office, closing the door behind him.

We'd stayed at the Masquerade until dangerously close to dawn, then returned to Chelsea in the limo Spider had rented for the night. We'd stripped off our clothes and fallen into bed together, where we'd slept intertwined, my head on his shoulder and one of my legs bent over his. I'd woken up to Spider making love to me, slow and sweet.

That night, Jared's father, Primus Darkman, had flown to New York and tried to throw his weight around. Karoly Kral, the Kral primus, had shut him down hard. Jared had snatched a guest from a Kral event, after all. Even his own people testified to that. Darkman Senior had put out feelers trying to locate me, but the Krals had told him I'd been staked while trying to escape from Jared, and Darkman had given up and returned to Vegas.

"What's up?" I glanced from Spider to the empty office.

"It's December first," he returned.

I scrunched my brows together. "And—?"

"And the thirty days are up. Our agreement is officially terminated."

Annoyed, I folded my arms over my chest. "I thought it ended that night you staked Grim and Troll. These last couple weeks, that was me in your bed, not your *thrall*."

We were mates, damn it. I'd never been happier, or felt more secure. Had it been different for Spider?

"I know, baby." His gaze tracked from my face to my crossed arms. "I'm doing this all wrong," he muttered and steered me to a drawer labeled 'Lark.' He jabbed a finger at it. "Open it."

What now? Still grumpy, I pulled open the drawer. My jaw nearly hit the floor. "That's—that's a lot of cash. Way more than we agreed on."

"One million."

I picked up a stack of hundreds and fanned the corners. "This is mine? All of it?"

"Yes."

I slapped the stack back in the drawer and closed it with a snap. "You think you have to *buy* me?"

He recoiled. "No! It's...security. You can take that money and walk out of here tonight."

I twisted away from him, hands on my hips. "Really," I said, my brows raised. "And you'd just let me go."

"Fuck, no." A muscle jumped in his jaw. "Did it feel like I'd ever let you go tonight in the shower? Or last night when I had you bent over the chair?"

Lust stabbed through me all over again, remembering. I swallowed. "No."

"Damn right, I won't," he said between gritted teeth. "Because if you leave, I'll be right behind you. But I want you to know you can." Something vulnerable flashed over his face. "I...I need to know you're staying because you want to. Not because it's your only option."

My heart pounded against my rib cage. For the first time, I *felt* how susceptible he was when it came to me, how he'd do anything for me.

And it scared him, but then, it scared me a little, too. The vulnerability went both ways.

Neither of us had brought up the M-word yet, but I'd bet that drawer full of cash that both of us were thinking about it. We were mates. The bond had already started to form. You don't sense another supernatural's emotions without it.

Now, I realized that he was trying to make a big gesture—that even the thought of losing me terrified him.

Wonder spilled into me like a cascade of fireworks. "Thank you." I interlinked my fingers around the back of his neck. "But you're crazy if you think I'd leave. I have a home and friends and you. You're stuck with me, Spider-Dude. And that drawer is the sweetest, most generous thing anyone has ever done for me. I don't need it, but that you thought of it means everything."

"I mean it." He slapped my bottom. "That money is yours to use however or whenever you want. And if you need more, just ask—or hell, take it. You're my queen, baby. Anything I have is yours." His dark eyes warmed, his expression so, so tender. "I love you, Lark."

I dug my teeth into my lower lip. It was the first time he'd said it aloud. "I love you even more," I managed to say around the lump obstructing my voice.

"That's not possible," he returned. His long fingers speared into my hair, tipping my head back. His teeth scraped down my throat, sending a hot thrill over my skin. "So that's settled. We should plan our mating ritual—Yule would be a good night, I think. Zayne can help."

I blinked, laughter bubbling up in me. "Did you just ask me to accept your mate bond?"

"No, baby." He nipped me beneath my jaw. "I told you."

I moaned and angled my head to the side, giving him better access. "I...don't think that's how it works," I managed to say.

"It does for us. Now stop teasing. You feel it. You know you do."

I shrugged a shoulder. "I wasn't sure."

"Because we haven't said it out loud. We need to speak the words in front of witnesses."

I pulled back so I could see his expression. "What about Amina?"

"She was never my mate," he said without hesitation. "Now that I have you, I know the difference. I loved Amina, but she wasn't my mate. You're it for me, thief."

My heart squeezed. He meant it. I felt his love and need wrapping around me like an extra pair of arms.

"You're it for me, too." I kissed him hard. "And Yule sounds like the perfect night to make things formal."

"Mm." He palmed my butt through my leggings. "Have I told you about this fantasy I have?"

"What's that?"

He walked me backward until the top of my thighs hit his desk. "You're a thrall and I'm your master."

I giggled. "That's a fantasy?"

"Quiet, woman. All I want to hear out of you is 'Yes, sir.'"

"Oh, that kind of fantasy."

He turned me around and bent me over the desk, shoving the bowl of diamonds out of the way. His hand landed on my ass. "Did I say you could talk?"

"Why do I always end up bent over the furniture?"

Another swat. "Because it makes you hot."

The heat between my legs proved his point. "Fair," I admitted.

He smacked me again. "Sir."

My inner thighs constricted. "Sir," I hurried to say.

"Good girl," he praised, and I smiled at the desk.

He peeled my leggings and panties down and helped me off with my shoes and socks. Next went my shirt. No bra, since Spider liked me without it.

Now I was naked, while he was fully clothed. Maybe we were playing at being master and thrall, but we were both invested in the fantasy, and acting it out in his office had made me so turned on I would've begged if he'd required it.

He guided me down onto the smooth gray surface of the desk again. I quivered, expecting another spank. Instead, he dropped to his knees and pressed a kiss to the curve of my ass where it was warm and probably pink from his smacks. He teased me with a finger, then his tongue, then twisted so his head was between my thighs and started eating me out, his finger toying with my puckered hole.

Waves of pleasure flooded me, one after another. I babbled something and pressed against the desk, arching my back, half of me trying to get closer, half of me trying to escape. He gripped my butt cheeks and kept me where I was. Sharp teeth sank into my inner thigh next to my pussy, taking a tiny sip.

"Fu-uck," I keened, and went up on my toes as an orgasm smashed into me like a wrecking ball, taking me apart so that it felt like pieces of me ended up all over the room.

When I came back to myself, I was lying on the table, my cheek and breasts pressed to the cold metal.

Spider rose to his feet. "Turn over."

I sucked in a breath and obeyed, watching as he reached behind his shoulders and dragged off his T-shirt in a single smooth, hot-as-fuck move. Then his pants and boxers were around his ankles and he was in me again, his hands pressing my wrists to the desk on either side of my head, his powerful body covering mine.

My pieces reassembled into a woman who felt so incredibly lucky. If I hadn't moved to New York... If Grimclaw hadn't sucked at being an alpha... If I'd refused to steal Spider's dagger...

Spider shoved into me, slamming me against the unforgiving metal. Then he did it again, and again.

It was raw and erotic and wild, and made me feel so wanted.

No, not just wanted. *Necessary.*

His gaze caught mine. "Who do you belong to?"

I tightened my thighs on him. "You."

"That's right." He pushed me again, then did this twist with his hips that made me gasp. "And I'm never, ever letting you go."

"No," I said, climbing toward another orgasm.

"Mine," he said.

"Yours," I said.

And in that moment, the mate bond snapped into place, pulling us together, stronger than anything I'd ever known.

Yeah, we'd speak the words, make it formal. Throw a party, celebrate with our friends.

But we were already mates. The bond was real, and it was ours.

Gabriel, Zaq and Rafe Kral have their own books!

THE DARK ANGELS (THE VAMPIRE SYNDICATE)
Three powerful brothers and the women they'd burn down the world to have...

They call us the Dark Angels: Gabriel, Zaquiel and Rafael.
We're brothers. Princes. Billionaires.
The richer-than-sin heirs to one of the world's most powerful vampires.
But we're not vampires, we're dhampirs.
Half-human, half-vampire, with panty-melting good looks.
The media love us.
Vampires hate us.
And Slayers, Inc. will do anything to take us down.

"A must-read!" ~*Paranormal Romance Guild*

COMPLETE TRILOGY NOW AVAILABLE!

- **TEMPTED** (Gabriel - a free Prologue)
- **PURSUED** (Gabriel)
- **CRAVED** (Rafe)
- **TAKEN** (Zaq)

~

Preview of Pursued

MILA

I'd been running so long that when the syndicate vampires finally caught up with me, I almost welcomed it.
Almost.

I was hungry. Painful, gnawing, can't-think-about-anything-else hungry. Somehow, I'd found myself in a Giant Eagle grocery store, doing something I'd promised myself I'd never do—shoplifting.

I slipped around a big man in striped shorts to snag a couple of avocados. A hand latched onto my wrist.

Not the big man in the shorts. Another man.

Cold lips touched my ear. "Security would be very interested in what you have in that backpack, cher."

A vampire, with a hint of New Orleans in his voice.

I froze, heart banging against my lungs so hard I could barely breathe.

No, no, no.

The big man rattled down the aisle with his loaded cart, oblivious. In the next aisle, a woman with a flat Ohio accent asked where the wine was.

I sipped in air. "I don't know what you're talking about."

"No?" The vampire started to unzip my backpack.

I closed my eyes, picturing myself busted in the produce aisle for three chocolate bars, a can of sardines, a hunk of cheddar and a bag of peaches.

"Stop it!" I twisted away, but he was right there.

Powerful fingers clamped onto my upper arms. "Then come with me."

I licked my lips and willed myself to calm down. A vampire can hear your pounding heart, turn your fear against you. "What's this about?"

Like I didn't know. Karoly Kral's men had been hunting me for three years.

"You'll see." The vampire turned me to face him. He was blond and inhumanly beautiful, with dark brows and a lean, sculpted face.

My gaze went to the black wolf tattoo on the side of his neck. A Kral Syndicate enforcer.

My blood chunked to ice.

A woman trailed by a kid in a dance leotard turned into our aisle.

The vampire glanced at them. His mouth curved. "Say you'll come, Camila. Or that pretty lady with the little girl in the tutu"—he jerked his chin at the woman and the kid—"will be food for me and my friend."

Bile filled my throat.

No, no, no.

But in my three years on the run, I'd learned some things about vampires, like that they tend to underestimate humans.

I hunched my shoulders, made my tone sullen. "I'll come."

For now.

The enforcer's hum of satisfaction raised fine hairs all over my body. He removed my backpack and dropped it on the floor. "You won't need this."

A peach fell out and rolled across the aisle. I stifled a moan.

Insane, right? To be worried about fruit when you're being kidnapped. But I'd lusted after those peaches like a teenager craves the one boy she can't have, my shrunken stomach grinding at the sight of all that sweet, juicy fruit.

The vampire put an arm around my shoulder and walked me out the doors. I slipped my hand into my back pocket and palmed the silver switchblade concealed there.

His scent was dark and earthy, like the deepest part of a forest. My chest constricted. I didn't want this man close to me —he made my skin crawl—but that familiar forest aroma made my insides knot with yearning.

Outside, dusk spread its wings over the parking lot like a malevolent black bat. The humid July air pressed on my skin, gluing my curly hair to my nape.

My gaze locked on the limo with tinted windows idling at the curb. Stupid, to let myself get caught out this close to nightfall, but it had been weeks since I'd seen one of the undead.

My captor hooked a finger into the waistband of my too-loose shorts. I'd lost weight, the past few months.

"You know what I am, right?"

I dipped my chin. "A vampire."

"Then you know I can outrun you without breaking a sweat."

"You *can't* sweat," I muttered.

"Exactly."

He caught my wrist in a tight grip and with his other hand, opened the limo door to usher me inside. Polite and slick as hell.

A frazzled mom, juggling a toddler and two bags of groceries, sent me an envious look, taking in the sexy vampire in the ten-thousand-dollar suit helping me into the limo like I was his pampered thrall, not his prisoner.

It's not what you think, I wanted to scream.

The vampire glanced at her—and I struck, releasing the switchblade and stabbing him in the ribs with the silver point.

He snarled and swore at me, but his grip loosened enough for me to wrench free. I sprinted across the access road—right into the path of a big, double-cab truck. I threw myself out of the way and continued across the parking lot, dodging shopping carts and gawking onlookers.

My car was unlocked—always. I'd learned even a few seconds could make a difference. I yanked the door open and scrambled inside. I hit the lock and started the car at the same time.

The ancient engine jerked, hesitated.

I turned the key again. "Come on, come on. You can do it."

I glanced around, lungs working in short, panicked bursts. I couldn't see the blond vampire, but I knew he was out there. A Kral enforcer wouldn't let me go this easily.

The engine stuttered.

I drew a sobbing breath. "Please, please, please..."

The engine ground to life just as fingers clamped on the rim of the door. On the other side of the window, the blond vampire appeared like something out of a horror movie. Long white fangs and dark eyes with a glowing blue rim.

All the spit left my mouth. The bright, glowing blue around his irises was a bad thing. Very, very bad. You didn't see blue rims unless a vampire was aroused—or furious.

A sharp jerk, and the rusted door gave with an earsplitting screech.

I slammed the car into gear, but he plucked me out of the seat by the nape of my neck like I was a runaway kitten. I snatched the switchblade off the seat as he reached across me to shove the gearshift back into *park*.

He set me on the pavement in front of him. I planted my feet and brandished the switchblade.

We faced off. But vampires don't play fair.

Blue-rimmed eyes captured mine. "Come with me, Camila." His voice held the force of compulsion.

I strained backward, resisting with everything I had, but I couldn't drag my gaze from his.

"*Now*," he commanded. "Drop the knife and take my hand."

"No." The word scraped out of my throat.

But he was too powerful for me. The switchblade clattered to the pavement and I took his outstretched hand like a freaking zombie.

Forgetting my car. Forgetting the switchblade at my feet. Forgetting everything but the compulsion to obey.

He speared his free hand in my hair, dragging my head back. He shoved his face into mine. "No more fighting. You will come with us."

Somewhere deep inside, I shrieked *no*, but my head bobbed up and down. "Yes."

The limo pulled up next to us. Inside were two other men: a human at the wheel with a boxer's bent nose and beefy arms, and another vampire, this one with dark hair and sleepy eyes, sprawled on the leather seat, long legs stretched out before him.

"Get in." My captor shoved me into the back seat.

The sleepy-eyed vampire shifted his body enough to allow me space on the seat beside him. "Camila."

I growled.

"I am Stefan," he said. He had an accent, too, but his was Central European—Russian, or some other Slavic country. "And that is Martin." He looked at the blond, who'd taken the seat on my other side, a hand to his ribs. "What happened?"

"Bitch stabbed me with a silver blade."

Stefan chuckled. "You will live."

Martin sent me a dark look. "No thanks to her. Lucky it didn't go deep."

The limo pulled out, leaving me sandwiched between the two lean, cover-model-gorgeous males. The forest scent filled the limo's interior. A vampire's way of enticing us poor, stupid humans to come closer.

I crossed my arms over my stomach, fighting down panic. I was weaponless, my only clothes my hoodie, T-shirt and cargo shorts.

On the other hand, I was still alive. Maybe these weren't the same vampires who'd been trying to kill me for three years?

We pulled onto the highway. "What do you want?" I asked.

"The crown prince has never forgotten you," said Stefan.

The crown prince? My heart skipped a beat.

It was Gabriel who'd sent them, not his father Karoly?

"Yeah?" Longing twisted through me. I scowled to hide it. "Then why scare the crap out of me by sending you two to snatch me? Why not just ask politely—you know, in the usual way—a phone call? A text?"

"Would you have come?" asked Stefan.

"No," I said flatly.

Silence.

You didn't say no to a vampire syndicate prince. Especially the crown prince.

"Besides," Martin said, "you're using a burner phone."

"Like you don't know the number." The fact that they even knew I had a burner phone proved my point. "So. What does he want?"

"Our orders were to pick you up," Martin said.

"And take me where?"

"New York."

I swallowed. The Kral Vampire Syndicate headquarters were in Manhattan.

"What if I don't want to go?"

Martin's smile was white. "What makes you think you have a choice?"

"Fuck you, too," I said, but fell silent as the limo took the exit for the airport.

There was no use arguing. They wouldn't let me go. I might as well save my energy for the upcoming confrontation with Gabriel Kral.

Because I couldn't stay with him, no matter how much I might want it.

I stared out the window as night fell over the flat midwestern countryside. In the past few years, I'd lived in four different states, always in small, out-of-the way towns with none of the money and glitz that attracts a vampire. Three months ago I landed in this aging suburb near Cleveland, and taken yet another dead-end, low-income job.

I'd barely saved enough to move into a basement apartment —a room, really, with a tiny kitchen at one end and a single pint-size closet—when the store manager called me into his windowless beige office and ordered me to shut and lock the door. He'd moved closer, licked his thin lips.

I'd known what was coming, and God help me, I'd almost

said yes. This job had taken me almost a month to find and I was down to my last fifty dollars.

But I'd refused and stood by the open door as I told him to go to hell, saying it loud enough that the ladies out front would hear me. Two days later, he fired me for being five minutes late to work.

The vampires were still scrutinizing me.

Another wave of longing washed over me. There was something so seductive about how a vampire watched a human.

Gabriel had watched me like that, his green eyes hungry, and I'd fallen into his lap like a ripe plum.

But I'd been young, then. Barely out of my teens and starry-eyed with love. I was older now, and harder.

My shoulders curved inward, the adrenalin surge that had carried me across the parking lot gone. Almost too exhausted and hungry to be afraid, and mourning the loss of those damn peaches nearly as much as the switchblade, my only silver weapon.

"Fine." I forced my spine to straighten. "Just tell me there's going to be food on this jet."

They did feed me on the flight to New York.

And I ate, even if I felt a little like beef-on-the-hoof being fattened for the butcher.

A pretty flight attendant handed me a menu and invited me to order anything I wanted. I started with three appetizers, then moved on to a salad of tender greens topped with cranberries and candied pecans. Next was crab-stuffed flounder with a side of herbed red potatoes that I washed down with what was probably an expensive white wine, given I was on a private jet.

The vampires slouched on leather couches, sipping wine and speaking in undertones to each other.

I was full now, but I stubbornly kept eating, only because I caught Martin's envious glance. A vampire can drink a glass of wine and maybe have a bite of food once every few days or so. Other than that, they have to stick to blood.

After a while, I'll bet it gets pretty damn boring.

A chocolate mud pie topped with whipped cream and shaved chocolate rounded out my meal. I held Martin's gaze as I forked up a large bite.

Eat your heart out, blood sucker.

We landed at La Guardia well after dark, and took another limo into Manhattan. My palms were sweaty now, all that rich food churning in my stomach.

Another limo conveyed us to the Upper East Side, a street right on Central Park that reeked of old money and behind-the-scenes power. Prewar apartment buildings. Carefully trimmed trees. Small rectangles of annuals surrounded by miniature black-iron fences. Even the trash cans were brand-new and of coated green steel.

The heat was still stifling as I exited the limo flanked by Stefan and Martin. They were silent now, cold-eyed. They marched me between two potted orange trees. One doorman let us in, and another pushed the elevator button.

The ride up was so quiet I could hear the frantic pounding of my heart. I pushed my back against the brass bar and stared at the shiny metal doors.

Gabriel.

Ironic, that a vampire prince had an angel's name. And not just any angel, but God's left hand man. Protector—and destroyer.

I should hate him for dragging me back like this. He'd sworn the decision was up to me.

But a small, secret part of me was excited. The part that still wanted him, no matter how wrong it was for both of us.

The elevator reached the top floor. We stepped out into an

apartment with high ceilings and a parquet floor polished to a golden sheen. The tall windows were made of that special dark glass that allows vampires to see out even on a sunny day. Right now, though, the view was of Central Park at night, its winding wooded paths dotted by lights.

Stefan and Martin escorted me through a big-ass foyer into a living room. The lighting was dim—vampires have eyes like cats—and the furniture elegant but comfortable. Butter-soft black leather, a plush red-and-black carpet, black metal lamps with shades shaped like tulips and lilies. I suppose if you live as long as vampires do, you appreciate comfort as much as beauty.

Four women in skimpy black dresses lounged on the couches or on velvet pillows near an unlit fireplace. Their necks were bare, the tiny marks from a vampire feeding barely visible. They would've been beautiful if not for their empty eyes. They smiled a greeting at the two vampires with me but remained where they were like the obedient thralls they were.

We entered a long gallery hung with dark, moody paintings that together were probably worth as much as the entire apartment building. I glimpsed the name Degas scrawled in the corner of a painting of a woman drinking alone in a bar. Another depicted a hazy river at sunset that even I recognized as a Monet.

We entered a library filled with wall-to-wall bookshelves. A tall, dark-haired man stood by a window, looking out at the busy street below.

A tingle went up my spine. *Gabriel Kral.*

My lover. My prince. And the heir to the Kral Syndicate.

Then I froze, hands fisted at my size. I tried to back up, but Stefan and Martin had ranged themselves behind me, a solid, immovable wall.

The man turned to face me. "You're not Gabriel," I rasped.

Order *Pursued* from your favorite bookstore!

ALSO BY REBECCA RIVARD

Thanks so much for reading!

Want to be the first to hear about my vampire romances and other steamy paranormal romance books? Sign up for my newsletter: rebeccarivard.com/newsletter

In return, I'll gift you with a free story.

THE VAMPIRE SYNDICATE

Sexy, gritty vampire mafia romance...

Tempted (Prologue)

Pursued

Craved

Taken

Fallen

Hunger

Thirst

The Vampire Kingpin

Learn more: rebeccarivard.com/vampires

VAMPIRE BLOOD COURTESANS

Steamy vampire romance set in Michelle Fox's Blood Courtesans
World...

Ensnared

Compelled

Learn more: **rebeccarivard.com/vampires**

THE FADA SHAPESHIFTERS

Dark shifters, seductive fae...

Stealing Ula (Prequel)

Seducing the Sun Fae

Claiming Valeria

Tempting the Dryad

Lir's Lady

Shifter's Valentine

Sea Dragon's Hunger

Saving Jace

Charming Marjani

Adric's Heart

Learn more: **rebeccarivard.com/shapeshifters**

ABOUT REBECCA RIVARD

USA Today bestselling author Rebecca Rivard read way too many romances as a teenager, little realizing she was actually preparing for a career. She now spends her days with vampires, shifters and fae—which has to be the best job ever.

Rivard's writing has received numerous prizes including the prestigious PRISM, the RONE, and the Paranormal Romance Guild Reviewers' Choice Award for both her Vampire Syndicate and Fada Shapeshifters Series. In addition, eight of her books have been awarded *InD'Tale Magazine*'s coveted Crowned Heart Review.

When she's not writing, she walks and bikes in the Chesapeake Bay area with her guitar-playing, storytelling husband. She loves exploring and is always on the lookout for mysterious castles, eerie cemeteries and other abandoned places that she can use as settings in her novels.